Praise For The Destination: Desire Series

"I loved this amazing, emotional love story... A tear or two became commonplace during some intense scenes. In Ms. Jordan's talented hands, the characters evolved naturally and realistically, flaws and all."
-Harlequin Junkie Reviews

"5 stars. My favorite in the series so far. I just loved the back story of this couple and it's just a different twist on a romance. Loved it!" *-Kristi Simonsen*

"This is an well written story, where you get invested in the characters and root for them to have their HEA...I cannot wait to see what comes next in this series. 5 stars" *-Gigi Staub*

"This was a fabulous story with great characters... one of the best I've read this year. I LOVED this." *-Jennifer McKenzie*

WILD FOR YOU

DESTINATION: DESIRE
BOOK 4

C. JORDAN

CJ BOOKS

Book cover by James, GoOnWrite.com

This work was originally published as an e-book in © 2015, with a second edition in © 2025.

First print edition 2025

contents

DeDicaTion

For all the fans who celebrated the life, love, and travel of the four amazing friends in this series.

For the Professor Moriarty and the Mad Madam M. Life as I know it would not exist without my best friends (though I only sleep with one of you).

For Grams. You are missed. Now, always, and forever.

CHaPTer one

Half Moon Bay, California

The final confirmation email had arrived.

It was official: she was booked on an adventure cruise through Alaska's Inner Passages. Three solid weeks of sailing, camping, hiking, kayaking, and ice climbing in some of the most gorgeous wilderness the US had to offer.

This was going to *rock*.

Even an hour later, a huge grin still curled Anne Kirby's lips. She did a little dance step as she crossed Main Street and bounced into the Moonside Café, where she was meeting her three best friends for their weekly dinner.

Karen pressed a palm to her burgeoning belly, using her free hand to wave Anne over. Anne slipped into the seat next to the blonde, where they faced Julie and Meg.

"What's up?" Anne asked. There was an air of tension over the table that made her a bit wary.

"Wedding planning," replied all three of her friends at once.

Yikes. There was a topic guaranteed to give Anne hives. Not something she was ever doing. No way, no how. Hell, no. Even if she ever took the fall for some lucky guy, she was eloping. Somewhere far, far away. Period. She shuddered to think of the mileage for drama her mother would get out of a wedding. Yep, she'd leave that pain and suffering to her little sisters, if they decided to do the full event.

A waitress came by to fill Anne's coffee cup, and she nodded her thanks.

"Back to our conversation." Making an agonized face, Karen glanced at Meg. "The ceremony is still a month away, girlfriend. *Look* at me. I'm huge and I still have seven weeks to go! I can't believe you want a woman who'll be eight-and-a-half-months pregnant as your maid of honor. Not that I'll upstage the bride in prettiness, but I might eclipse you if I turn sideways."

Anne snorted but tried to cover it by taking a sip from her mug. Not that she fooled anyone—her friends knew her too well for that.

"I don't care," Meg replied, her tone emphatic. "I want my friends there with me, even if we have to roll you down the aisle. We're keeping it short, so you won't have to be on your feet long. Besides, I think Finn might die if we did a big, formal, dragged-out ceremony."

"Please," Anne shot back. "That man would crawl over broken glass for you. If you wanted a long, fancy-ass ceremony, he'd let you have it."

A satisfied grin tugged at Meg's lips, and a happy sighed soughed out. "Yeah, he would. I think I'll keep him."

"Blech." The annoyed noise was out of Anne's mouth before she could stop it, and her three friends stared at her. She waved them away. "You guys are just so disgustingly in love. *All three of you*. It's nauseating."

Julie's look was sly. "Jealous, little orphan Annie?"

Oh, now there was a surefire way to piss her off. The fact that she had bright red hair had led to more teasing in her childhood than she cared to recall. Orphan Annie, Anne of Green Gables, Carrot Top, Big Red. The list went on, some more perverted and insulting than others. Her hair couldn't even be a nice shade of auburn like two of her three younger sisters. Nope, Anne's was red. In-your-face *red*.

She scrubbed a hand over her short locks and glared at Julie. "Don't be a jerk."

Julie opened her mouth to retort when Meg poked her in the arm. "Quit antagonizing."

"But that's what I *do.*" Julie's eyes widened. "Someone has to egg you guys on or we'd never have any fun."

"Too bad. You'll adjust," Karen replied unsympathetically, patting her rounded belly.

Movement rippled beneath the surface, which always fascinated and horrified Anne at the same time. She set her palm next to her friend's and felt the baby kick. "The belly alien lives."

The creepy, ominous tone she used made Meg and Julie chortle. Karen just rolled her eyes. "Yes, and the belly alien wants feeding. So unless you want me to sic him on you, you'd better flag down the waitress so we can order."

Anne arched an eyebrow, glancing across the table at her friends. "You know, I think she means it. Pregnancy has turned her cannibalistic. The belly alien's terrifying bloodlust is taking over her body."

Meg flagged down the waitress. "I think it's vampires who have bloodlust, not cannibals."

"Yeah." Karen's smile was not at all reassuring. "Cannibals like their food cooked. They roast 'em live over an open fire first."

Julie raised a finger in the air, her tone turning as pious as any priest's. "Note that I am not the one antagonizing here."

"You're such a good girl," Anne cooed. "We'll be sure to tell Lukas to reward you tonight."

"No need." Julie's grin was positively sinful. "I'll tell him myself."

The waitress appeared with a breadbasket and took their orders. Karen fell on the rolls like she'd never eaten before in her life. She moaned, closing her eyes.

"Okay, while she has a private moment with the bread..." Anne let that thought trail off and reached into her messenger bag. Pulling out the printed email, she slapped it on the table. "Check that out."

Meg and Julie leaned forward. After a moment of silence, Julie squealed. "No way! You did it?"

"What?" Karen craned her neck to see. "Oh my God, you finally booked a trip to Alaska? You've been saying you wanted to go there forever!"

She threw her arm around Anne's shoulders for a quick hug, and Anne couldn't stop a stupid grin from spreading across her face. While she'd been on a million weekend trips to Yosemite, Big Sur, Mount Shasta, and the Sierra Nevadas, she'd always had to stay close enough to home so she could ensure her younger sisters got to school Monday morning. But her youngest sibling had just finished up her freshman year in college and had a summer job in San Francisco, which meant Anne was free to leave town. She'd be back in time for Meg and Finn's wedding at the end of July and the start of the school year in mid-August. She was a gym teacher at the local middle school, so these summer months without any responsibilities were a first. Normally, she spent the whole time refereeing the squabbles between the diametrically opposed personalities of her sisters. But not this year.

"Three whole weeks," she said with relish. "I was going to take the ten-day trip, but they had a last-minute Memorial Day sale and I jumped on it. Three. Freaking. *Weeks.*"

Her friends squealed and enthused and asked questions and Anne could feel a little of the dissatisfaction that had plagued her lately begin to fall away. Yes. This was exactly what she needed. Time to get the hell out of Dodge.

Meg hesitated for a long moment. "I hate to ask but...what did your mom say?"

Ah, yes. Her mom. There was a topic guaranteed to burst her bubble. Dinah Kirby was the biggest drama queen who'd ever lived, and Anne had no idea how she was going to break this to her in a way that wouldn't cause a meltdown. Her mom was codependent on a level that suffocated Anne. It hadn't been so bad with her sisters there to help deflect, but now?

Anne sighed. "I didn't want to tell her until I had something to tell. Until I pushed the buy button, I wasn't sure I was going to do it. So that's what I get to do after dinner."

Julie's expression was compassionate. "My couch is available if she goes atomic on you."

"Thanks. I'll be fine." Or at least, Anne hoped she would. Dinah and she rarely fought—mostly because Anne kept her mouth shut—so this might be a novel experience. Not a *fun* experience, but a novel one. "Really, it'll be fine."

Meg cocked her head. "As long as you don't let her drive you into staying in Alaska forever. I expect you to be back for my wedding." She poked a finger in Karen's direction. "If pregnant lady and the belly alien can't escape, you can't either."

Kicking back in an exaggerated pose of relaxation, Anne folded her hands behind her head. She grinned. "Honey, I'm not just going to be back in time for the wedding, I'll be back in time to make sure you have a bachelorette party you'll never forget."

"If it's anything like the one she threw for me..." Karen's voice trailed off, her eyes rounding with horror.

Anne just let her smile widen in a way she knew would worry them. As it should. Really, there was nothing quite so fun as yanking her best friends' chains.

D espite her bold words about everything being *fine*, trepidation filled Anne as she unlocked the front door and walked into the four-bedroom ranch-style house she'd shared with her family since she got hired at Half Moon Bay Middle School. The Kirbys had moved more times than she cared to count, but once she'd had steady income of her own, she'd made sure her sisters had a stable home.

Rustling noises came from the kitchen, and Anne followed the sound to find her mother kneeling on the floor amidst a pile of packing materials, lipstick tubes, and makeup cases.

Dinah glanced up with a smile. "The company released their new line today. The colors are *gorgeous*."

At the moment, her mom was trying her hand at being a cosmetic salesperson. She was throwing a party this weekend for her friends and some of their neighbors. Anne hoped it was more successful than the time Dinah tried to be a real estate agent, or a massage therapist, or a waitress, or a delivery truck driver. Yeah, right. She'd been fired from more jobs than most people knew existed. And she was such an utter flake that it was pretty doubtful this new jaunt into beauty consulting would go anywhere but failure either.

Frustration bit at Anne. *Why* couldn't Dinah hold down a job like a normal person? *Any* job? Why was Anne always the one who had to pick up the pieces and hold everything together?

Jesus, but she needed this vacation. After sucking in a deep breath, she let it out slowly. "Hey, Mom. Have a minute to chat?"

Dinah nodded, running a pencil down a list of inventory. "I just need to check off the persimmon lipstick. Ah, here it is. Okay, what's up?"

Best to just be up front with it. Prevaricating only gave her mom time to get suspicious, paranoid, and panicky. "I'm going to be taking a trip."

A pause. Dinah blinked. "To where?"

"Alaska."

"Did you meet a man on the internet?" A huge smile wreathed her face, and she pressed a hand to her chest, tears beginning to well. She whispered, "I'm so happy for you, baby."

"Um..." Anne shifted from foot to foot, acute discomfort knifing through her. As usual, her mom had gone sideways with a conversation, and there was no way to get back to normal without upsetting her. It was pretty telling that the only human being on Earth who regularly rendered her speechless was her mother. "Uh...there's no guy. I'm going on one of my outdoor trips. Kind of."

Her mother's expression quivered, and then fell into a frown. "You're going camping? In Alaska?"

"They have some really pretty wilderness there. Orca whales, mountains, trees... I'll get to see it all. And take lots of pictures." Okay, not that Anne really cared about the photos, but her sisters loved the nature shots she took when she went hiking.

Dinah's mouth tightened, her eyes narrowing. Ah, yes. The suspicions had been aroused. Now came the guilt. "When do you leave? How long will you be gone?"

"At the end of June." Anne went to the fridge and pulled out a bottle of water. "There was a flash sale online. I'll be gone for a little over three weeks."

"Why do you have to go so far away? California has great wilderness." Her mom waved her hand as if encompassing the whole state.

Aiming for a casual shrug that felt more like a spasmodic jerk, Anne said, "I know, but the girls are all working or interning this summer and they're in college now, so I figured I could take some time for myself."

"What about me?"

You're a grown-ass woman and you need to start acting like it. Your youngest child is in college, for fuck's sake. Anne swallowed those bitter words. "What about you?"

Tears pooled in the older woman's eyes. "I'll be lonely."

So, get a cat. More words she didn't say. If her mom got a cat, Anne would the one taking care of it. Much like she'd been the one taking care of her little sisters. Not that she held that against her sisters. She was glad she could be there for them. She did, however, hold it against her mother. Drama queen I-am-so-helpless-please-save-me extraordinaire. Anne had found it harder and harder to keep her mouth shut since her baby sister, Camille, left for college a year ago.

For once in her life, Anne wanted something that was *just* for her. Call her selfish, but she'd been raising someone else's kids since age sixteen, when her dad died and her mom went from lovably flaky to completely unreliable with bouts of unstable thrown in for extra fun. She deserved a break.

The problem was, she'd expected things to improve once all the girls were out of the house. But, nope, her mom was still living with her, still only sporadically employed. And it was all Anne could do these days not to lash out and say the horrible things that would damage their family forever. Because the girls would get dragged into a fight between Dinah and Anne, and Anne wouldn't hurt them for the world.

So she needed to get out. Just for a while. Just...*out*.

"I'm going to check my gear so I'm ready when it's time to pack." She turned around, exited the kitchen, and walked down the hall to her room.

Her mother trailed after her, sniffling. "But...I don't do well on my own, Annie. You know that."

"So go and stay with Aunt Terri." Anne glanced back.

"Arizona is awful this time of year. Hotter than hell." Dinah twitched the limp hand that was still holding her inventory sheet. "And I'm trying to start my new job."

"Well, that should give you something to keep you busy and focused." Yanking her massive backpack out of the closet and dumping it on the bed, Anne avoided meeting her mother's eyes. But she could still feel Dinah's gaze boring into her skin, and knew her mom wanted her to feel guilty. Anne threw up her hands. "I don't know what to tell you, Mom. You're an adult and I expect you to be able to entertain yourself for a few weeks."

Okay, so maybe that crossed the neutral line, but if you can't look out for yourself at fifty-seven, it's probably not a good sign.

"Annie." The whine in her voice grated on Anne's last nerve.

She looked at her mother squarely. "You know I don't like to be called that. My name is Anne."

Dinah flinched as if Anne were a monster who'd kicked a puppy. The older woman's chin trembled, and her voice dropped to a throbbing whisper, "This house will be so big and empty without you."

"The trip is non-refundable, Mom. It was a sale." Anne took in a slow breath, steeling herself, and her tone hardened. "Even if it wasn't, I'd still go. There's absolutely nothing you can say or do to stop me. Period."

Her mother's lips parted in shock. As mouthy as Anne was with everyone else, more often than not, she did whatever she had to do to appease her mother. It had always been necessary in order to save her sisters from more drama. But there was no one left here except the two of them.

Dinah gave an offended huff. "You...you..."

"I...what?" Anne pulled her favorite hiking boots out of the closet. She needed to inspect her pack, sleeping bag, and all her footwear to make sure they were still in good shape for the trip. Her gear was well-used, so if she needed to replace anything, she wanted to have time to break the new piece in before she left. She grabbed her rock-climbing shoes to check them over, trying to ignore the quivering indignation emanating from the doorway.

"How can you just abandon me like this?" Dinah snapped, going from pathetic sniveling to towering fury in the blink of an eye. "You're supposed to think about your mother!"

"You're the mother, and I'm the child. Your child needs this vacation. You should think of your child's needs." *For once.* "You'll be in your own home. You can visit your friends. You can throw extra makeup parties. Do whatever you want, Mom. *I'm* going to Alaska."

Okay, so that last bit came out more fiercely than it should have, but Anne tightened her jaw against the urge to give in to whatever her mom wanted in order to head off a meltdown at the pass. Not today. She was not giving up this trip. She'd been eying these excursions to Alaska for *years*, wishing she could go, wishing she could manage more than a long weekend away without worrying about her sisters' health and safety. Not that their mom had ever been abusive, but she had no problem with giving the girls cupcakes for every meal. Not to mention how often she didn't bother with or remember to pay the bills. Assuming she'd held a job long enough that she could afford to pay them.

Anne was tired of being the adult in this relationship. Seriously, was this all she had to look forward to? Being her mother's keeper?

Is this it?

That was the question that had been plaguing Anne lately. She'd watched her sisters move out of the house, seen her best friends find love...everyone was moving on with their lives and Anne was still here. Going to the same job every day, still living in the same house with her mom. She felt trapped. Stuck.

Was this all there was to her life? Day in and day out, year in and year out? Was she going to grow old, look around, and still be asking herself: *is this it?*

"I'm going to Alaska," she reiterated, the words colder than the climate she was heading for.

"Fine. If you feel like you have to get away from me." Her mother's voice wobbled, sliding back to pathetic, and Anne was entirely unmoved. It was exactly the kind of emotionally manipulative thing her mom always said to get her way, but Anne didn't think she could give in this time without losing a little bit of her soul.

She'd always found peace and rejuvenation on her trips out into the wild. This time, she needed as big a dose of that as she could find.

CHAPTER TWO

Juneau, Alaska

The cold bite of air hit Gabe's skin as he left his cabin and stepped out onto the deck of the *Alaskan Adventure*. Even in late June, the temperatures could dip to freezing at night. The day was headed toward sunset, so the thermostat was dropping fast. He tugged on a hoodie over his thermal shirt and walked over to the rail. Most of the crew would be gathered in the dining room socializing and sipping coffee, and he'd join them soon. Caffeine was a necessity, but he wanted a few minutes of quiet solitude before the next group boarded for their cruise. He wouldn't have much peace for the next twenty-some days.

"A new day, a new set of tourists." Oliver grunted, slumping against the railing beside Gabe.

"Yep." He grinned over at the ship's captain. The two had been friends for the five years Gabe had spent his summers leading the off-boat expeditions on the *Alaskan Adventure*. He stretched his arms over his head, loosening up his limbs.

Oliver scratched his bearded jaw. "Maybe there'll be hot babe in this bunch."

"Right." Gabe slapped his friend on the back. "And she'll be traveling with her new husband on a honeymoon trip, so all you can do is drool and wish you were him."

The other man snorted. "Only the crazy ones come on their honeymoons. Hubby can keep the crazy. I don't need it."

Gabe laughed. "That's the spirit."

The men lapsed into silence, gazing out over the harbor. Though the *Adventure* was a cruise ship, it was a small one. They had the berth space for forty passengers, plus the crew. Considering the big cruise liners could hold over twenty-five hundred passengers, the *Adventure* was a tiny canoe by comparison. But Gabe liked the smaller operation, liked that he got a chance to know people during the weeks onboard. Of course, that closeness also meant it was harder to avoid the annoying characters, but he generally got along well with everyone.

A satisfied grin stretched his lips. He'd spent far too many years in the Silicon Valley rat race, making buckets of money as a programmer, but toiling away until he was practically living in the office. His bosses had approved of his work ethic, but after the first flush of success wore off and the grind never seemed to get any easier, he'd started to hate every minute of it. On his thirtieth birthday, he'd looked around, realized life was too damn short to spend it miserable, and walked away without a backward glance.

That had been five years ago, and he didn't have a single regret. He'd signed on to guide every kind of backpacking, hiking, biking, rock climbing, paragliding, ziplining, sailing, and rafting outdoor adventure all over the world. He made pennies compared to his previous salary, but he was more content than he'd ever imagined being. It was a trade-off that had been well worth it.

Oliver's brows drew together. "Isn't this the tour your parents are coming along for? Or is it the next one?"

"This one. They should be with the group boarding." Gabe's grin spread. His older brother had come along on several of the excursions he'd led over the years, but this was a first for his parents. While they'd all been worried about his career switch, after they'd gotten over their initial shock, they'd been remarkably supportive.

He was a fortunate man on so many levels. Great job, great family. Yeah, life was good.

With his mom and dad along, this should be an awesome trip.

"Here they come." Oliver straightened, glancing down at his watch. "They're early."

A trail of laughing, bouncy people were headed toward the gangway. Some had already thrown themselves into the vacation mindset, and he could see an almost giddy freedom in their expressions. Gabe could easily pick out those who were still wound too tight, who *really* needed a break from their lives.

Well, they'd come to the right place.

He hadn't spotted his parents yet, so he leaned forward to try to find them. He ran his gaze along the line of tourists. A tall woman who towered over her companion caught his eye, and he blinked. He took in her willowy length. She had a shock of hair so red it looked like living flame as the strands danced in the breeze. A laugh burst from her rosy lips, and her mouth formed into a wicked smile.

Wow.

That smile was enough to send equally wicked thoughts spinning through any heterosexual man's mind. She had slight curves, but the wind flattened her top against her and cupped every one of those curves like a lover. He could almost see the outline of her beaded nipples, and while he knew it was a reaction to the cold, he couldn't stop the automatic response of his body.

Damn, but he hoped this particular hot babe wasn't here on her honeymoon. Because he wanted to meet her.

Oliver nudged him in the ribs, bringing reality back into focus. "That guy looks like an older version of you, so if that's not your dad, I think your mom was lying to you about the mailman."

"Yeah, that's my dad." Gabe raised an arm and waved.

He had to fight a wince as he realized he'd been so focused on the redhead that he'd overlooked the fact that it was his mother trotting along beside her. His father walked a few strides behind the women.

"I'm going to the bridge." Oliver slapped him on the back and turned away. "Enjoy the family reunion."

The moment they boarded, his mother dragged the redhead along to come greet Gabe. It looked like he'd get to meet her immediately, but with his parents watching the interaction. Good news, bad news. *Ah, well.*

His mom glanced up at the redhead. "See, I told you I made good-looking sons. My older boy is just as hot, but he's married already."

The tall woman laughed and the sound was smoky and sexy. Nice. She looked even better up close than she had from a distance. Her eyes were sparkling with mirth, and they were so pale a brown they were almost pure gold.

He held out his hand. "Hi, I'm Gabe Warren. Nice to meet you. And don't let my mom fool you. She has to be diplomatic, but I'm much better looking than my brother."

His mother chortled and his dad rolled his eyes.

"Anne Kirby." Those golden eyes crinkled at the corners, and as she took his hand, her gaze did a quick flick over his body. Oh, yeah. That was interest flittering across her expression. Nice. A little grin tilted up one side of her mouth, a hint of flirtatiousness, but nothing overt. Since his parents were standing right there, he appreciated her restraint. Her skin was amazingly soft, but her handshake was firm and no-nonsense, and he liked that too.

"I'll be leading the outdoor excursions on this trip." He flashed his best smile at her.

Her voice was just a little throaty. "Well, I'm planning to take advantage of those."

Maybe it was completely unprofessional to be thinking it, but he was hoping she'd be taking advantage of a lot more than his guide skills. The cruise company didn't have a non-fraternization policy with co-workers or guests, thank God, though it was awkward as hell to be considering that in front of his family members.

"I'm going to go find my cabin and get settled." She gave an easy wave to his parents. "Peggy, Vince, I'll see you both for dinner?"

"I think we'll see you at the ship orientation session first." His dad pulled the itinerary out of his pocket to show her. Always on top of every detail, that was Dad.

"Great. I'll meet you there." Anne bumped her shoulder into his dad's.

The three Warrens watched as she disappeared into the ship. Then his mom swung around, her expression full of the devil. "So you like her, huh? I totally called that. Your dad owes me ten bucks."

Gabe arched a brow. "You were betting on this?"

Dad grinned unapologetically and shrugged. "Like you didn't hop right into the betting pool with us when we were guessing when your brother would finally pop the question."

"True enough," Gabe agreed. He scooped his mother up, lifting her off the ground for a moment and rocking her. "Hey, you."

"Hey, you." She squeezed him tight. "It's so good to see you, baby."

"You too." He set her down and ruffled her hair like she was a kid. She ducked away and swatted at him. He chuckled and turned to his father, who hauled him in for a back-slapping bear hug. "Glad you're here, Dad."

His dad leaned back and gave a pointed glance at the door Anne had just gone through. "Yeah, though we may be messing with your game plan."

Gabe shook his head. "No plan. No game. I'm glad you're here. I've been looking forward to this for a while and nothing will mess with that."

He meant it too. As attractive as Anne Kirby was, his family had always been a top priority. He wasn't going to ignore them in favor of a woman he'd just met. With any luck, he could multitask. He'd have to, considering he was onboard to work.

Interesting times ahead. His favorite kind.

W ell. A sexy guy as a tour guide and she already knew she liked his parents. Anne had never had that mystery solved so fast. Then again, that information was usually only useful after a few months of dating to see if she liked the guy enough to bother finding out if she liked the parents.

Of course, said tour guide was also a little on the scruffy bum side of life with his stubbled chin and a job that wouldn't last past the end of the season. She winced at that. Exactly the kind of guy her mom would *love*—just as big a flake and just as unable to hold down a real job as she.

Too bad.

Gabe Warren was attractive, Anne would give him that, *and* he'd managed to make her laugh within two minutes of meeting him. He looked like a big, sleepy lion, all shaggy sun-bleached golden hair, tawny skin and cat-green eyes. The way his thermal shirt and jeans had fitted his body told her he was ripped. Like, holy mother of God, let-me-see-you-naked-please because that was the hottest bod she'd ever laid eyes on. If nothing else, he'd be some exceptional eye candy on this voyage.

She grinned as she stowed her stuff in the tiny postage stamp of a room. It was actually one of the ship's larger cabins, where she had a queen size bed and a room all to herself. Many of the cabins were shared and only had two twin size beds crammed into the same space. But that was pretty typical for a cruise ship—boats had limited square footage to work with.

She didn't want to stay cooped up in her room though. All her tension had started stripping away the moment she'd hopped off the plane in Alaska. The cool air filling her lungs had a sharper bite than the ocean breeze from the California coast she called home. There was the scent of lingering snow on the wind—something she never dealt with in Half Moon Bay. It was so different, such a nice break from the pressures of her life. She hadn't been able to stop grinning, and when she'd heard Peggy making a dirty joke to Vince as they disembarked the shuttle to the harbor, Anne hadn't been able to hold in a chuckle.

Peggy had glanced back and winked and, well, Anne was pretty sure she'd made a friend for the trip. And the quiet humor in Vince's gaze made her like him on sight. She'd also noticed a couple of other athletic women on the shuttle, so she was guessing they might be joining her on the more physical activities and would be less into the nature walk, bird-watching stuff.

It would be nice if she wasn't the only woman going on those off-boat excursions. Not that she couldn't keep up with the guys, but a little gender balance made for a better trip.

Never one to sit still long, she finished putting everything away, grabbed her camera, and left her cabin to trot up the stairs to the main deck. Her friends and sisters would want some pictures of day one, so she might as well snap a few before she had to go to orientation.

She worked her way around the small cruise liner, taking a few photos of the harbor, the city skyline and the channel that would connect the ship to a series of inlets and islands along the way. The boat rocked a bit, and she braced her legs apart to remain balanced, but kept her eye on her camera's viewfinder so she could get the angle she wanted.

"Pretty, isn't it?"

Gabe Warren's deep voice rumbled directly in her ear, and she startled, her heart slamming against her ribcage. She whipped around and clapped her free hand over her chest. "Shit! Sneaking up on people is not cool, dude."

"Sorry." His eyebrows rose. "I didn't mean to sneak."

Considering he'd been practically nibbling on her earlobe before he spoke, she sort of doubted his sincerity. And the thought of him nibbling any part of her body sent a little shiver down her.

He's a deadbeat like Mom, Anne. Get a grip.

After a beat of silence, she said, "Don't worry about it. Did you want something?"

When his grin went absolutely naughty, she realized her wording mistake. *She* was usually the one with a wicked comeback. That he'd managed it without saying a word sent a dart of annoyance through her, especially since her pulse was still galloping. From being startled or from being this close to the hot, disheveled tour guide? She didn't think she wanted to examine that too deeply.

Dredging up the no-nonsense tone she used with her students, she said, "I'm sure you have work to do, Mr. Warren. Don't let me keep you from it."

Turning away, she refocused on getting a good picture.

"Nope, I'm pretty free at the moment. And I'm Gabe—Mr. Warren is my father."

Awareness prickled between her shoulder blades as he continued to stand there, just close enough that she felt the body heat coming off him in waves. Why was he so close? Why did that awareness turn to warmth in the pit of her belly? Damn. She sighed and lowered her camera.

"Am I bothering you, Anne?"

Yeah, like she could admit he bothered her. That would certainly give him an advantage. Though she wasn't even sure how this encounter had become competitive. Other than she was always competitive. Maybe he was too, which meant pursuing even a mild flirtation with him was out of the question. Fighting to keep the upper hand would not help her relax and be all zenlike on this vacation, which she desperately needed. Though it *was* too bad. She'd enjoyed their little back-and-forth when they met. And he was damn pretty. His earlier comment about his brother meant he knew it too, more's the pity.

She glanced over her shoulder. "Do you have a reason for invading my personal space, Gabe? I'm guessing harassing passengers isn't in your job description."

He took an infinitesimal step back, a gleam of challenge in his gaze. Oh yeah. This one liked competition too.

Her heart tripped and beat a little faster, and she had to fight her own instinct to answer that unspoken challenge. She should not engage. "I'm going below deck. Excuse me."

"You don't want to do that," he replied implacably.

"Yeah, I really do." She tried to step around him, but he feinted and dodged so she couldn't. She growled, "What the *hell?*"

He set his hands on her shoulders, tightening his grip when she tried to jerk back. "You *don't* want to go down there. One of our passengers yarked in the dining room and then all the way down the hall to his cabin."

Oh. Ew. She scowled up at him. "You could have just *said* that right up front."

He leaned in a little, dimples digging deep grooves into his stubble-covered cheeks. "But then I wouldn't have gotten to touch you."

It took a lot of effort not to grin...and not to kick him in the shin. He was equal parts cute and obnoxious, which should not be as appealing as it was. The heat of his fingers began to seep through her clothes, and she had to suppress a shiver. She cleared her throat. "You can stop now."

His thumbs moved in a slow sweep against her collarbones. "Stop what?"

Her breath caught and she tried to cover it with a cough. "Touching me."

"Where would the fun be in that?" He backed her up a few steps, until she felt the press of the railing on her spine.

She tilted her head to meet his gaze. She was a tall woman, used to towering over others, but he made her feel petite. She wasn't sure if she liked that or not. "Aren't I supposed to be the one having fun here? Of the two of us, I'm the one on vacation."

"You're not having fun?" Pure innocence radiated from him, and his eyes widened in surprise.

Yeah, right. He didn't do the innocent look very well. Then again, neither did she. She had to suppress another grin.

Letting his hands fall from her shoulders, he set one on the railing just to her right. She wasn't trapped, because she could slide left, but she certainly felt *surrounded*. Their chests almost touched, and if she took a deep breath, her breasts would be pressed to his well-defined pecs. Her nipples went hard and her mouth went dry. The burn of chemistry hit her, and reluctant attraction exploded into something much more dangerous. Tingles went down her skin, and she opened and closed her mouth, but nothing emerged.

This was insane. She was never speechless with men, but her tongue was stuck to the roof of her mouth, pure desire pouring through her veins. He was absolutely the wrong man to be fascinated by.

It irritated her that *his* voice managed to be easy and conversational. "So, what made you want to spend your vacation on a boat in Alaska?"

Forcing herself not to think about her traitorous hormones, she responded, "I like being outdoors."

"Good choice, then." His gaze moved over her face, coming back to stare into her eyes as if he could see all the way down into her soul. "Let me guess...corporate America, looking for an escape from the stressful rat race of a job you don't really like very much, but the money is too good to quit?"

Since her mother was more of a life sentence than a job duty, she didn't even have to lie when she made an obnoxious buzzer sound and said, "Nope. Wrong on all counts. But thanks for trying to diagnose me, O Camper Guru."

He ignored the guru jab and shook his head. "Not diagnosing. Just recognize the overstressed signs a lot of our guests have when they first get here. A little *too* overjoyed to be here. Almost relieved, you know what I mean?"

Well, that observation hit the nail directly on the head. "Any stress I have is not currently job related. I'm a PE teacher. I'm on summer break."

His eyebrows went up, and he straightened his arm a bit, pushing away. "So, where's the stress coming from? Family? Boyfriend?" A hesitation. "Husband?"

That made his interest clear, didn't it? Not that he'd been subtle so far. She smirked. "No husband."

He leaned slightly closer, his green eyes crinkling at the corners. "Boyfriend?"

"Nope."

"Thank God," he said feelingly.

She laughed at that one, she couldn't help herself. It was rare she met anyone as outrageous and mouthy as she was. Then again, his mom fit into that category too, so he came by it honestly. "You think it's going to matter to you if I'm single?"

"A man can hope." His lids dropped to half-mast, somehow looking slumberous and smoldering at the same time. That was exactly the kind of look a woman wanted to get across a pillow in the morning.

"Aren't your parents on this trip too?" She'd hate a man who ignored his family. Family was the most important thing in Anne's life. She'd sacrificed a lot to keep hers together and happy.

"Yes, they are, and I can't wait to spend time with them." His smile showed genuine affection laced with wry humor. "And apparently they like you and intend to keep you around. Mom and Dad always bring me the *best* presents."

She bit her lower lip so she wouldn't give in to the grin that wanted to form. "You have really nice parents."

"I'm incredibly lucky." There was no mockery or sarcasm in his tone. Then his expression softened. "Are you?"

"Excuse me?" Because, of course, the word "lucky" associated with this man took her brain to dirty places, but they were talking about parents, right?

The way his dimples flashed told her he knew exactly how she'd misinterpreted him. "If your stress has nothing to do with your job or your significant other, that leaves your family, right? Does that mean you're not quite as lucky as I am with my parents?"

How to answer that question? She sighed.

His eyebrows rose. "That bad, huh?"

Shrugging, she looked away. "It's complicated, and not really something I want to talk about with someone I barely know."

"A shame." He tilted his head to try to meet her gaze again. "Maybe by the end of the trip, you'll be willing to tell me about it."

She cocked a hip and propped her hand on it. "So, Camper Guru, this attitude you have...would you call this confidence or arrogance?"

"A little of both, probably." He winced. "You're not going to let the Camper Guru thing go, are you?"

"Why?" She felt an evil grin curve her lips. "Am I bothering you?"

Because that might be the answer to getting him to go away. The problem was, she was far too attracted to him, and he was exactly the kind of guy she always avoided. She didn't do unreliable slackers, because, hello, *her mother*. It would be just her luck if she fell in love with the first one she bumped uglies with, and spent the rest of her life supporting his freeloading ass. He could hang out with Dinah all day. Wouldn't that be great fun?

So, if she couldn't avoid being attracted to him—and on a ship this small, short of hiding in her cabin, there was no way she could evade him if he wanted to find her—maybe she could poke him with the proverbial stick often enough that *he* avoided *her*.

Game on.

CHAPTER THREE

T hree days later, hell, yes, she was bothering him.

And he'd reached new levels of pathetic.

Gabe had had a non-stop hard-on since he'd had her pressed up against that railing, and as she showed no sign of wanting to do anything other than argue with him about every-damn-thing, it was unlikely he'd get relief with anything other than his own fist in the foreseeable future. It was just too bad he found her mouthy attitude a turn-on. Then again, it wasn't as if he didn't enjoy going toe to toe with her.

Pushing away those thoughts, he focused on steering the boat toward shore. The El Capitan Cave tour awaited. He'd volunteered as a secondary guide to tag along after the official US Forestry Service guide, who would take them through the twisting system of caves. Normally, he let one of the newer guys on the crew handle this excursion since Gabe had been on it a dozen times already. Except he knew Anne had signed up and, thus, here he was.

Yep, a whole new level of pathetic. He was only grateful his parents had decided to sleep in, so he wouldn't be harassed.

He throttled down the boat so it came to a gentle stop as they bumped against the dock. After hopping out, he tied the watercraft down and turned to help the passengers.

"Let me give you a hand, Bridget." Gabe smiled at the forty-something soccer mom who'd gotten up early to come on this fieldtrip. Minus her husband and teenage boys. She'd been cracking jokes with Anne since they'd boarded the boat.

"Um… Thanks." Bridget stammered and blushed when she took his hand to let him haul her onto the dock.

Anne, of course, bounced out with no assistance, propped her hands on her hips, and took in a deep breath while she looked around.

Mist curled over the water, up the shore, and around the old growth trees. Between those trees wound a wooden staircase that went up the mountainside until the steps eventually disappeared into the fog. Gabe had to admit, the beauty of the area never ceased to awe him, no matter how many times he'd been here.

The smile on Anne's lips and the dreamy look that crossed her face told him her thoughts might have flowed in a similar direction. Damn, she was lovely. He was getting addicted to seeing her smile. He'd watched her mobile features and easy laugh at every meal for the past three days. His parents didn't have an ounce of subtlety between them, so they'd made sure to rope Anne into sitting with them, throwing her together with Gabe. Not that he minded, and she'd been good humored about it, which made him like her more.

"Okay, folks. It's about 40 degrees in El Cap Cave, and dark as pitch. Make sure you've got your coat, sweater, or other layers to keep warm. Does everyone have their flashlight?" The five people on the tour all nodded and showed him their flashlights. Of course, Anne took the opportunity to shine a beam right in his eyes. He grinned and shook his head. He was definitely getting her back for that later. "Excellent. Let's go meet with the Forestry Service guide."

Within fifteen minutes, Gabe was bringing up the rear as they all huffed and puffed their way up hundreds of stairs to get to the mouth of the cave. He could feel it in his glutes, so he knew those who weren't in the kind of shape he was would be hurting tonight. Since Anne and Bridget were right in front of him, he couldn't complain about the view. Anne had one hell of a nice ass—round and perfect and made for a man's hands. *His* hands, if he had anything to say about it by the end of this cruise.

He kept one eye on the group as they worked their way up the mountainside. Eventually, Anne and Bridget passed some of the slower climbers while Gabe had to stay behind to make sure the stragglers got to the top safely. Too bad about the loss of view, but he took his job seriously.

Once they reached the platform outside the cave opening, the Forestry Service guy started on his spiel about the depth of the cave, the geological history of the area, and safety measures they needed to take because of the moisture that dripped from the ceiling and made the ground slick.

Gabe's gaze went to Anne, as it always seemed to whenever she was around, and he watched a wistful expression cross her face. Wistful? Anne? The emotion seemed so out of character, he sidled sideways to close the few feet of distance between them. "You okay?"

She blinked and looked at him. "Sure, I guess."

"You just looked...like you saw something you really wanted but couldn't have." And he had difficulty believing she'd feel that way about the skinny grad student giving them the tour.

She shrugged sheepishly. "When I was in high school I wanted to be a forest ranger. I applied to the Forestry Management program at Oregon State and everything."

"You didn't get in?" He slanted her a sympathetic glance.

Her face scrunched up. "I got in, but my dad died my junior year and someone had to help my mom with my little sisters, so I double majored in Kinesiology and Mathematics at San Francisco State University instead."

There was a lot more to that story—he'd bet his entire savings account on it. "That's a bit of a jump from forestry. They didn't have an ecology program or something?"

Her shoulder twitched. "Not a ton of reliable jobs for that in Half Moon Bay. I knew I'd have to stay in town until my sisters grew up. Nora was in kindergarten when Dad passed, and Hazel and Camille weren't even in preschool yet." Her gaze met his, her voice matter-of-fact and without a hint of regret. "I knew teachers would always be needed, so I got certified for both Math and Physical Education. Drove up to SFSU for classes every Monday and Wednesday, came home, then worked Tuesday, Thursday, and Friday to help my mom make ends meet."

The fact that she was philosophical about the kind of sacrifice that most people would have refused to make left Gabe blinking in shock. From what little he knew of her, he understood that she'd be defensive if he praised her. So instead, he asked a question. "If you were helping your mom out, how did you afford college?"

"My grandmother—Dad's mom—died just after Cami was born and left all of us girls money to pay for university. And that was the *only* thing we could use the funds for." She took a hard hat from the guide and plopped it on her head, giving Gabe a jaunty smile. "There wasn't enough for anything too fancy or expensive like Harvard, but it paid for a state school, which is where all of us have gone."

Setting his own hat on with one hand, he pressed the other palm to the small of her back and urged her toward the cave. "There's a huge age gap between you and your sisters."

She nodded, ducking through the entrance into the cold dark behind the rest of the group. They all clicked on their flashlights. Anne glanced back at him. "Eleven years from me to Nora. Then two more to Hazel and one-and-a-half more to Cami."

So his voice wouldn't echo, he whispered back, "Why the gap? Do you all have the same mother and father? Not halves or steps?"

She hesitated. "My parents split up when I was a toddler, and I shuffled back and forth between them until I was nine and they remarried." Her mouth tightened. "I...think my dad took her back for me."

His chest squeezed in sympathy. Her mom sounded like a real piece of work, and he said a silent thanks to his own mother for being her obnoxiously amazing self. He and his brother had been incredibly fortunate to have both their parents. He reached out a hand and squeezed Anne's shoulder. "Sounds like it was a rough way to grow up."

"Other people have it way worse. It's not like we were homeless, starving, or abused." Her muscles tensed under his palm.

Defensive, as he'd suspected, but he was going to say it anyway, "Giving up your dreams for your family is a big deal, whether you want to admit it or not. You're pretty awesome, Anne."

Her shoulder hunched. "Thanks. My sisters were worth it."

"Let's catch up to the others." He stroked a hand down her arm, just for the pleasure of touching her. "It's far too easy to get lost in the switchbacks of this cave system."

"Okay." The relief in her voice made him smile. For all her opinionated bravado and sass about every taboo topic under the sun, she was self-conscious about having her merits pointed out. An interesting contrast. Then again, everything about her seemed to interest him. Maybe more than it should, but he'd worry about that when and if it actually became a problem.

The guide had stopped and the group gathered around him to hear about the formation of the rocks over time and the types of artifacts that had been found during exploration. Dripping water echoed through the cave, and the flashlight beams caught the droplets and made them sparkle as they fell.

The group walked for almost two hours in those caves, Gabe bringing up the rear, Anne always one step ahead of him, and Bridget flitted around to chat with everyone. Every so often, the USFS guide would stop to point out a geological feature or give them historical tidbits. Gabe tuned most of this out since he'd heard it many times before, enjoyed the beauty of rocks, and made sure to watch the group so no one wandered off. They were on their way out when the guide made the last stop before they left the cave. Gabe grinned. When they continued on, he made sure to direct his flashlight into Anne's eyes just as they turned.

"Hey!" She planted her hands on her hips.

"What?" He arched an eyebrow. "You think I didn't notice you doing that to me earlier?"

Her teeth gleamed white in the murky darkness. "You're supposed to rise above that sort of thing, Camper Guru."

"Sorry, sugar. I'm not a saint by any stretch of the imagination." He swept another quick glance over the tourists in front of them. Anne and he lagged behind a few steps. He lowered his voice and leaned closer to her ear. "And if you keep calling me that stupid name, I might have to spank your ass."

He felt her shiver, and a curl of lust filled his belly.

"Sorry, sugar," she mimicked him, though her voice came out a bit breathy. "I'm not into that *Fifty Shades* shit."

Laughing, he shook his head. "It's too bad for me that I'd really like to know what you *are* into."

She twisted at the waist to say something when her foot slipped. His heart seized, but he snapped his arm around her waist. He hauled her against him to keep her upright. The side of her hip hit his groin and her helmet collided with his, which sent his flying off to bounce against the rocks. For a moment, they hung there in silence, nothing but the sound of their harsh breathing and the dripping water coming to his ears.

A shudder ran through her and her gaze met his. "That was close."

"Yes."

She tried to step back, and her foot slipped again. Reflexively, he tightened his grip on her, and she clutched at him. Her breasts flattened against his chest, her thighs pressed to his, and he clenched his teeth on a groan. He'd wanted her in his arms for days, but this wasn't how he'd imagined it. Still, the feel of her slight curves molding to his body made heat rip through him.

"Are you all right?" he asked, his voice a low rasp.

Her head came up and her gaze fastened on his lips. She licked hers, and he couldn't hold back the groan this time. Tension jumped between them like a live wire, electrifying the moment. Instead of pulling away again, she tightened her fingers on his shoulders. It was like inviting a starving man to a banquet. He had to taste her. He just had to.

His hand lifted to bracket the nape of her neck, keeping her near, and he felt the tickle of her short hair against his fingers. "Say no."

A laugh huffed out of her and her eyelids dropped to half-mast. "I can't."

"Good," he growled and then captured her lips.

This was no slow exploration, but a fiery taking. His tongue plunged into her mouth, and the flavor of her exploded over his taste buds. Coffee and sweet strawberries she'd had for breakfast, as well as something that was pure female. Pure Anne. His palms roamed down her back, memorizing the feel of her slender form.

She shoved her fingers into his hair and twisted them tight. The slight pain just sharpened the pleasure pounding through him. Her tongue dueled with his, her teeth nipped at his lower lip, and his erection was so hard it ached. He ground himself into the soft cradle of her thighs, craving more, craving *her*. She arched into him, a strangled little sound bursting from her.

Jesus, it was all he could do not to drag her to the ground. Desperate need dug vicious claws into him. If he'd thought he'd wanted her before, it was nothing compared to how he felt when he finally had her pressed against him. White-hot lava poured through his veins. He bit back a groan, curving his hands over her backside to pull her tighter into him. Her breasts crushing to his chest while she wriggled to get even closer was mind-blowing.

A rumbling crash sounded, an agonized shriek ripped through the cave, and Gabe's heart slammed against his ribcage. Anne and he jerked apart, lungs heaving. Bending, he grabbed his hard hat and slapped it back on his head and then they hurried toward the sound. They found Bridget and the Forestry Service guide sprawled amidst a pile of large rocks a few yards from the cave entrance. The other guests huddled around them.

"What happened?" Gabe asked, striding over to kneel beside the fallen people. Damp mud immediately oozed into his pants where his knees touched the ground. He ignored the discomfort. Bridget had her leg wedged between a couple of boulders. He had to crouch forward to get a better angle to check on her condition.

The guide scrambled to his feet and winced. "I stopped to say something and she ran into me. We both went down on the rock. Slipped in the mud."

Pale and a little wild-eyed, the guide wrung his hands. Gabe would guess that while the kid had had first aide training, he'd never dealt with an actual injury.

"It does get muddy," Gabe agreed. One clear look at Bridget's leg and he could tell it was broken, possibly in more than one place. He ran his hands over her other leg and she cringed when he got to her ankle. One broken and the other possibly sprained. Awesome. He glanced at the USFS guide, keeping his voice calm so he didn't spook the kid. "You need to radio this in, make sure there's a way to transport her to the local medical clinic. This isn't going to be something we can deal with on the ship. We're going to need a stretcher to carry her out of here. Got it?"

"Right. Yes. Got it. I-I'll go do that." Unclipping the walkie-talkie at his belt, the guide scurried from the cave.

Gabe swept his gaze over the rest of the group. They all looked shell-shocked and a bit panicky. "Why don't you all go outside and wait with him for help? I'll shout if we need anything."

Sheer relief crossed a few faces, and they hurried to obey the voice of command. Likely they were grateful to be given *something* to do.

Anne knelt beside him. "Hey, Bridget."

The other woman's smile was thin, a trickle of sweat sliding down one temple. "Man, I had to fall on my ass in front of the cute one."

"The Cute One, huh?" Gabe examined the rocks, trying to find the best way to get her leg free without causing more pain or, worse, further injury. "That's way better than what Anne calls me."

Bridget started breathing shallowly, in through her nose, out through her mouth. "What does Anne call you?"

"Camper Guru," Gabe and Anne said together.

The supine woman snorted. "That's not nice, Anne."

"Nice is a four-letter word." The redhead flapped a dismissive hand. Her tone was light, but he saw the worry in her gaze.

"Yeah, don't go dropping the four-letter n-bomb or your mom will wash your mouth out with soap." Gabe flashed a grin at Bridget before he moved around to the other side of the boulders. He was guessing the larger of the rocks had moved during the fall, and its tip rested against the smaller rock. The gap in between was where Bridget's leg lay. She was lucky her limb hadn't been crushed, and the way the big rock quivered when he touched it said that its position was precarious at best. They needed to move Bridget now, or crushing was still a serious possibility. But there was a clear path between the boulders, they'd just needed to slide her out. Without tipping the big rock. Fan-fucking-tastic.

"My mom is dead," Bridget replied, pain pinching her features tight.

Gabe reached out and unlaced her tennis shoe, loosening it as wide as possible before he slipped it off her foot and handed it to Anne. He kept up the light banter with Bridget, trying to keep her distracted. "Well, *my* mom's on the cruise with us, and she'd be happy to wash people's mouths out as a mom-stand-in."

Anne nodded. "She'd do it too. Peggy's *nice* like that."

Bridget managed another weak smile. "The two of you are like watching a gag reel."

"You're welcome," Gabe and Anne chorused.

He met Anne's gaze and jerked his head for her to come around to his side of the boulders. He spoke in her ear, little more than a whisper, "The top rock is going to fall, and there's no good way to push it without risking her. I'm going to pull her out. Can you watch the rock and her foot from this side and help me maneuver?"

She nodded, her brows drawn together in concentration.

"Thank you. You're amazing." And she was. Totally steady and unsqueamish so far. He pressed a quick kiss to her forehead and then returned to the injured woman. "All right, Ms. Bridget. We seem to be in a rock-and-hard place situation, so we're gonna slide you free and get you out of this drippy cave before we all turned into drowned rats."

"Am I going to be okay?" she whispered.

"Absolutely," he replied firmly. Whether she would or wouldn't be was beside the point. Right now, he needed her calm and as confident as possible that everything would be just fine. "Okay, we're going to do this slow and easy. Ready, Anne?"

"Ready."

He slipped his forearm under Bridget's torso, lifting her slightly. She wrapped one arm around his neck, and set her free hand on the ground. "I can help you scoot me."

"Excellent. You're doing a fantastic job. Here goes the Drowned Rat Brigade." She laughed, just as he'd intended her to, and then he began moving her before she could think about it too much. The anticipation of pain only made it worse in the end.

He inched her little by little, and had to roll her slightly to get her foot through the gap. Her breathing turned heavy, low whimpers and sobs occasionally breaking out, but overall, the woman was a trooper. When her leg finally made it out, Anne came around and pushed the big rock away so it couldn't tip in their direction.

"Thanks," he said, nodding as calmly as he could. Only now did he feel the cold sweat that stuck his shirt to his back, the mud sliming his arms and legs, the icy drips of water from the ceiling. There seemed to be more of it coming down in this spot, which was probably the catalyst for the fall in the first place. He drew in a steadying breath. "Right, then. Let's get you bundled up in a blanket, toss you on a stretcher, and get the hell out of this hole in the wall."

Bridget swiped a hand over her damp eyes, then lifted her chin. "Toss me anywhere, Camper Guru, and you'll be a dead man."

"Now look what you've done." He poked a finger at Anne. "You're a terrible influence."

Both women chuckled, thankfully. Now he just needed to get them down this mountain in one piece.

I t took another two hours to hike Bridget down those eleven million steps and get her loaded in a waiting ambulance, which took her into town. Her husband was also waiting for them, and Gabe's parents had volunteered to watch their kids while they went to the medical center.

For Anne, the experience was...eye-opening. Gabe had managed to corral the three other tourists in their group, get the USFS guide's butt in gear, and deftly handle Bridget's injuries. He joked with her, kept her distracted, but he did exactly what he should to deal with a case like this. He was rock solid, unruffled, in control, and that kept everyone else calm.

Anne was impressed, and she wasn't a woman who impressed easily. She did her best to help him, carried the other end of the stretcher and kept up the light tone he used with Bridget, but he didn't *need* her there. Without her, he'd have had the Forestry Service guide carry the stretcher and he'd have been just fine. Not that Anne felt superfluous, but it was actually kind of nice not to have to be the one who projected the calm, in-charge, take-control attitude for others. She did it all the time for her students, for her sisters, for her mother.

Combine that with the first kiss that all other first kisses would now be judged by, and her determination to keep him at arm's length seemed futile. If she were brutally honest with herself, she'd admit it had been a losing battle since the moment she met him, but today had been a serious turning point. Maybe he was a vagabond, but he wasn't an irresponsible drama king who expected others to take care of everything. Watching him handle this crisis had shifted her view of him in a way that couldn't be reversed.

Bridget's husband went with her in the ambulance and Gabe took the tour group back to the cruise ship. The captain met them when they came aboard. Gabe had to fill out paperwork over the incident, and since Anne had been involved in the rescue, the captain wanted her statement of what had happened as well. Another forty-five minutes were blown on that fun.

Gabe dragged a hand down his face as they stepped out of the captain's office into the hall. "If we hurry, we can catch the tail end of lunch."

Her stomach rumbled an emphatic agreement with that suggestion, and she slapped a hand over it. "I need to wash my hands at least—though I really need a shower—but I'd rather be fed and kind of grubby than clean and starving. Or will they let me take it back to my cabin?"

"I could probably talk the kitchen staff into it, just this once."

She patted his shoulder. "Such a useful man."

His expression was comically startled. From the compliment or from her touching him? Then he blinked and turned to lead the way to the restroom. Anne scrubbed down as best she could, but the dining room closed for a few hours between lunch and dinner and she wanted food. Now. Exiting the bathroom, she ran into Gabe on her way to the dining room. Once there, they found a subdued trio of young teens sitting with Peggy and Vince. They stood up the moment Gabe and Anne entered, looks of worry on their faces.

Despite the fact that he had to be as sweaty, dirty, and tired as Anne was, he sat down with the kids and explained what had happened, reassuring them that their mom would be okay. He didn't get into any gory details or get overly technical with the medical jargon, but he didn't lie to them either.

Again, Anne was impressed. Other passengers gathered around to hear about the drama, and soon they had a large audience. While everyone was still asking questions, Anne rose and quietly fetched a tray with two cups of coffee—black, the way both Gabe and she preferred it—and a couple of ham sandwiches and bowls of chicken noodle soup. She brought the laden tray back to the table and slid Gabe's portions in front of him. He cast her a quick smile and dug in.

People turned to Anne and started asking her questions too, and she and Gabe managed to eat in fits and starts. She was more than ready to escape when she sucked down her last bit of coffee. Gabe seemed willing to stick it out and stay as long as everyone wanted him, but to hell with that. She stood up and grabbed the arm of his jacket, tugging him to his feet.

"Okay, folks. Gabe and I need a shower *desperately*. We'll see you all at dinner." She slanted a glance at his parents. "Let me know if you need anything in the meantime."

"We'll be fine," Vince replied easily. He patted Bridget's youngest boy on the shoulder reassuringly. Peggy nodded her agreement and shooed them away.

"Later, all!" Keeping her grip on Gabe's sleeve, she pulled him out of the dining room and down the hall. It wasn't until they'd reached her cabin door that she realized Gabe wasn't supposed to shower in her room.

Unless she wanted him to.

That thought floated through her mind, a temptation she didn't think she could resist. Not anymore; not after what she'd seen of him today. Not after that kiss. She wanted him, and maybe this wasn't going to be the kind of happily-ever-after relationship her friends had found, but she was a practical soul. Sometimes you took what you could get and enjoyed it for all it was worth. She grinned. Gabe was a pretty damn good consolation prize, especially if their naked chemistry was as good as the fully clothed version. She was guessing it was even better.

"Anne?" he asked, his voice a low rumble.

She blinked back to the present and met his green gaze squarely. "Do you want to come in?"

One side of his mouth quirked upward. "You know I do. Are you sure that's what you want?"

She cocked an eyebrow. "I wouldn't have asked if I wasn't sure, Warren."

A full-blown grin flashed across his face. "Good, because it would have really sucked if you backed out of that offer."

After using her cardkey to unlock the door, she grabbed the front of his jacket and hauled him into her cabin. His rich laughter warmed her insides, and then she shoved him back against the closed door.

She pressed herself into the muscular planes of his big body, making them both groan. Her nipples tightened, and goose bumps shivered down her limbs. Ah, yeah. Chemistry. "Let's try this again without the drippy cave and hard hat."

His hands framed her hips, pulling her tight into the swelling length of his erection. "Yes, please."

A chuckle trickled out of her as she brushed her mouth over his. It was like an electric current flowed from his skin to hers. A little tingle coursed down her body and heat followed in its wake. Very nice. She flicked her tongue out to slide along the seam of his lips. They parted for her, and she plunged into his mouth. Gabe and she fought for control of the kiss, nipping, biting, and sucking. The stubble on his chin rasped across her face, but it just added to the sensations rolling over her. Fire built within her, higher and hotter until she wanted to sob. The taste of him was perfect, and she pushed closer, wanting more contact but frustrated by the bulky layers of clothes they wore. She fumbled with the zipper on his jacket and wrenched it down. A quick tug and she had his thermal shirt free of his pants. Then her hands were on his bare skin.

He felt even better than he tasted, hot satin stretched taut over steely strength. She stroked over the hard slab of his abs, up to his well-defined pecs, and then circled his nipples. A shudder wracked him, and his fingers shifted to dig into her ass. His leg inserted between hers, and the muscles in his thigh flexed against her, rubbing over her sex. Her body throbbed and she felt a rush of moisture flood her core. *Oh God. Oh. God.* He shoved his fingers into her hair, bending her head back so he could deepen the kiss. It was wild, both of them breathing raggedly, their bodies grinding together.

She felt flakes of mud crack off her cheek and neck as they moved, and the sensual spell broke. She slowed down and pulled her mouth away from his. As much as she wanted to use him as her personal jungle gym, it was a bit gross to consider wallowing on her clean bed this way. "I hate to say this, but I really do need a shower. I'm disgusting."

He grimaced, glancing down at his mud-splattered clothes. "Yeah, I know what you mean. I don't want to stop, but...do we really want to call housekeeping and explain why they need to come change your sheets?"

She snorted. "Mud and bodily fluids—it's how all the popular kids relax these days."

Eyes narrowing in consideration, he tilted his head. "Showers on this ship aren't built to fit both of us."

He was right, she realized. The stall barely fit her alone, and Gabe wasn't a small man. She arched her hips into his and felt his erection jerk. Nope, not small *anywhere*. "That's too bad, really."

"I disagree." He gave her a little push toward the bathroom door. "I am seriously going to enjoy watching you get all naked and soapy."

She made a wickedly pleased hum in the back of her throat. "I'll be sure to make the show worth your while."

Putting extra sway in her hips as she moved, she grinned when he issued a tortured groan. She stripped out of her clothes, feeling the burn of his gaze as surely as if it were a physical touch. Liquid heat poured through her, and her inner muscles clenched in anticipation. It took all her willpower not to say to hell with the filth and jump him. Instead, she flipped on the knob and stepped under the hot spray. He filled the doorway of the bathroom, his arms crossed over his brawny chest as he watched her. The open door let the steam out into the bedroom, so they could see through the glass fairly clearly, see how they affected each other.

Every moment became erotic, every inch of her skin sensitizing as she lathered soap between her palms and slid them over her body. Her nipples pebbled to the point of pain, and she wanted his hands and mouth on them. She turned away from the spray and worked shampoo into her hair, then leaned her head back to let the water rinse the soap away. Rivulets flowed over her face and down her neck and shoulders. She slipped her fingers up her stomach, over her breasts, and into her hair to help get the shampoo out.

"God, that is the sexiest pose I've ever seen," he growled.

Opening her eyes, she saw green fire in his gaze. A flush of lust ran beneath his tanned skin and his chest rose and fell in quick pants. He still looked like a lion, but now one who hunted its prey. A shiver went through her at the thought. She was more than ready for him to pounce.

"Why don't you undress while I finish up?"

He shrugged out of his jacket and whipped off his untucked shirt. Bending over meant he could unlace his boots and kick them aside. His khakis came off so fast she was surprised he didn't end up with fabric burn on his legs. And, then, there he was in all his naked glory, and wow, he was even more built than she'd guessed. A light dusting of golden curls stretched between the flat discs of his nipples and arrowed down to below his navel. His shaft was a hard, thick arc that made her mouth water. She wanted to slide her tongue down the long, smooth length of him and suck him in her mouth.

Leaving the water running, she stepped out of the shower and grabbed a towel. "Make it quick, Warren. I don't want to wait."

"You don't have to tell me twice, Kirby." He swatted her butt as he slipped past and hopped under the spray.

She made a face at him and he winked back. When he ducked under the water, she got an amazing view of the most fabulous ass she'd ever seen on a man. She dried off slowly, letting herself look her fill as he moved. Heavy pecs, broad shoulders, a tight six-pack of abs and muscular thighs. She might drool. And his body wasn't even the best part of his physical perfection. No, it was his sinful smile that made her heart pound the hardest.

Leaning back against the doorjamb, she let the towel drop to the floor unheeded and just watched his hands move. Heat spiraled within her, and she pressed a palm to her belly. His gaze burned into her, and she let her fingertips drift down her midriff until she could dip into the thatch of hair between her thighs. His eyes widened and a strangled noise erupted from him.

She chuckled, the sound low and smoky. "You're taking too long, Gabe. I guess I'll have to get started without you."

The shower shut down a second later. He didn't even bother drying off, just stepped out and hauled her into his arms. His mouth slanted fiercely over hers, his tongue shoving between her lips. The fire within her exploded into an inferno, an uncontrollable need that made her dig her nails into his shoulders. He backed her toward the bed, and they went down in a tangle of limbs. She moaned at feeling the exquisite weight of him on top of her, and the dampness of his skin glued them together. The rough silk of his flesh, the crisp curls on his chest stimulated her flesh. She skated her hands over the flexing muscles of his back, into the delineated valley of his spine.

He dipped down and closed his mouth over her nipple. A gasp straggled out of her, and her back bowed. His stubble burned into the sensitive skin on the underside of her breast, and when he bit the tight tip, she cried out in utter want. She parted her legs and wrapped them around his waist, trying to get him where he could do the most good. "Now, Gabe. Inside me. Now."

The blunt head of his shaft rubbed along her slick sex, and she lifted her pelvis in invitation.

"Shit." He froze over her.

"What?" He was *stopping?* He had to be kidding her. She was going to kill him.

A muscle ticked in his jaw, but he moved his hips away. "I don't have any condoms with me. I mean, I have some in my room, but not on me. Do you?"

"Shit." She threw an arm over her eyes, her body throbbing in unrequited lust. "I'm dying here."

"We can't have that," he teased. When she lifted her head to glare at him, his grin was as roguish as a pirate's. "I'll just have to get creative."

He nudged her legs farther apart and slithered down to settle his torso in between them. He parted the lips of her sex, and blew a stream of air against her hot, damp core. Moaning, she squirmed while he chuckled darkly. Oh Jesus. He was going to—

Her lungs seized when he shaped his lips around her clit and sucked hard. Pinpricks of sensation shivered up and down her skin. His fingertips stroked over her wet flesh, circling, toying with her until she writhed on the mattress. Her heart pounded, beads of sweat gathering on her forehead to trickle down her temples. He plunged his fingers into her, filling her, stretching her.

"Gabe!" Her fists balled in the comforter, and she could feel orgasm building, like a rising tsunami wave that threatened to consume her.

But she didn't want to just lay back and take what he was giving her, she wanted to participate, wanted to make him feel like he was going to die from pleasure too.

She slipped her fingers into his damp hair and tugged. "I want to taste you, Gabe. I want—"

He groaned and maneuvered around so she could do just that. They lay on their sides facing each other upside down. Her top leg curled over his ribs, leaving her open for his exploration. The tip of his erection brushed against her lips, and she parted them to take him in. The musky scent and taste of him made her whimper. She slid her tongue down the length of him, using her hands to work his shaft in the same rhythm his hands and mouth set for her. He groaned and quivered, his hips pushing his shaft deeper. The combined sensation was enough to fry her nervous system. She was so close to the edge of oblivion, and she wanted to take him with her when she went flying. She drew on him harder, flicked the tip of her tongue against the bulbous crest. The way he jerked and gasped told her how much he liked that, so she did it again. And again.

In response, he hooked his fingers inside of her and rubbed over just the right spot. It was more than enough to make her break.

They came at the same time, groaning as climax exploded over them. Stars burst before her eyes as she sucked him, as her body tried to turn itself inside out. Rhythmic pulses squeezed her sex around his thrusting fingers, and great shudders wracked his form. They continued to work each other, wringing every last drop out of the experience. He seemed as unwilling to stop as she was, and aftershocks of orgasm quaked through her. Euphoria hit her in a blinding rush, and her entire body tingled. She sighed, letting the sweetness of it flood her. There were long moments of silence broken by the sound of their bellowing lungs and the whoosh of blood in her ears.

Finally, he pulled away, scooting around until he lay on his side next to her, his head propped in one hand. "You okay?"

"Ah, yeah." She flopped onto her back and let out a long, satisfied breath. "*That* is how an O-face is supposed to be."

A belly laugh rolled out of him. "Thanks, I think."

"You're welcome." Somehow she found the energy to lift a hand and pat his arm.

His gaze slid over her, then he frowned at her chest. She glanced down and saw the abraded flesh on her breasts. He rubbed a thumb over his chin, the short hairs making a scraping sound similar to sandpaper. "Sorry about that."

She huffed. "Did I complain?"

"Not that I noticed." He shrugged. "But I'm not at my most observant when a gorgeous woman has her mouth on my favorite body part."

"Well, if I didn't complain, don't apologize." *Duh.* She didn't add that last part, but she was pretty sure he heard it anyway because he snorted.

"Uh-huh. Still. I didn't mean to hurt you." He dropped a light kiss in the valley of her cleavage.

"I think I'll survive," she said drily. "But you can make it up to me later. With condoms."

CHapTer Four

G abe strode into the dining room with a lot more energy than he should have after a day like today, but getting one's rocks off in spectacular fashion with an incredibly smoking hot woman could do that for a man. He grabbed a tray and loaded up at the buffet stations. The menu rotated on a seven-day schedule, and it was salmon and mashed potato night. Cheesecake for dessert. A cup of coffee completed the meal, and he turned to see if he could find his family.

Yep, there.

Anne already sat at a table with his parents and Bridget's teenage boys. Actually, he wasn't sure the youngest qualified as a teen yet. He looked maybe eleven or twelve. The oldest of the three hadn't quite gotten over his gawkiness, so Gabe would peg him at maybe fifteen. He would have assumed those three would be back with their own parents instead of his, because he'd already heard that Bridget and her husband had returned safely to the ship. Despite the cast on one leg, she'd told the captain her family was going to finish the cruise. She'd spend her time enjoying the lounge chairs on board while her guys adventured.

Gabe set his tray at the one empty space left at the table, conveniently located next to Anne. As he sat down, she glanced at him with a smile, then did a slight double-take. He stroked his fingers over his clean-shaven jaw. Her grin turned absolutely sinful. He quirked his eyebrows, but neither of them said a word. She went back to her conversation with his father and Gabe glanced up to see his mother eyeing him speculatively. He took a sip of his coffee to cover his expression. Mom was wily, and still had the ability to read him like a book no matter how old he got. While he had no issues with people knowing he'd slept with Anne—and hoped to do it again very soon—his parents would meddle, and he'd rather avoid giving them the excuse. Also, he hadn't discussed with Anne how public she wanted this to be. She wasn't shy, but that didn't automatically mean she wanted to advertise her affairs.

Her arm brushed against his when she forked a bite of fish into her mouth. Goose bumps broke over his flesh, that electric awareness running through him. Watching her chew and swallow was a lesson in erotic torment as he vividly recalled the feel of her lips on his body. He jerked his gaze away before his pants grew uncomfortably tight.

A deep sigh drew his attention across the table. Bridget's youngest had a look of abject misery on his face. Gabe's eyebrows rose. "What's up?"

The kid took a swig of his soda. "My mom is sleeping in their room, but we were too loud and woke her up, so Dad told us to go for a walk. We did that until dinner, but I think we should maybe stay busy until bedtime."

Well, that explained how they'd ended up with the Warrens for dinner. Gabe glanced around the table. His parents looked a little tired, but a full day of babysitting high-energy teens could do that. Even though it was going to suck to miss out on a potential evening with Anne, Gabe smiled at the boys. "Why don't you just hang out with me?"

His mother protested, "We can—"

He just gave her a look. Whether she liked it or not, the retirees needed a break. She sighed and met his father's gaze. Dad shrugged and nodded, then took a big bite of mashed potatoes, signaling his unwillingness to discuss it further. He agreed with Gabe on this one. Mom pursed her lips and returned her attention to her meal.

Anne piped up. "I can stick around too, if you like."

Okay, so he wasn't going to get any sexy time with her, but he'd take any time he could get. He *liked* her. She could annoy him faster than anyone he'd ever met—and that included his family, which was saying something—but she also made him laugh and made him think. Two very large indicators of people he enjoyed being around.

"Sounds good, thanks." He squeezed her shoulder just for the pleasure of touching her. Then he addressed the boys. "We've got a games room, and I think they're playing a movie in there tonight."

"What movie?" The oldest teen perked up a bit.

Gabe winked. "Whichever one I decide to put on. Want to help me pick?"

The middle kid made a face. "We've played all the video games though. We have those ones at home."

"But there are board games too," Anne interjected with a challenging lilt to her voice. "Bet I can beat you at Monopoly."

The kid narrowed his eyes. "Nuh-uh."

"We'll see, won't we?" Her shoulders moved in a delicate shrug.

They finished up dinner and dessert, said goodbye to his parents, and trooped the kids over to the rec room. The place was mostly empty of passengers, who seemed to have turned in early. Crowds weren't as much a problem on smaller cruises like this one, which Gabe liked.

He also learned that Anne was *amazing* with kids. Of course, she made her living as a PE teacher with children around this age, so she had experience, but the evening wouldn't have been the same without her enthusiasm. The boys got swept up in her fun, and they spent several hours playing board games, but then she broke out her secret weapons. Charades, Hang Man, and Forfeit. He'd played the first two before, but in Forfeit, she'd take something from each player and then demand a particular stunt be performed before they could get their forfeit back. This was an instant hit with the boys because she was wickedly creative in her stunt demands.

Of course, he'd also found himself sitting through most of the game with no shirt on because she'd claimed it as his forfeit item. She'd taken her sweet time working her way through the boys' items. The flash of desire in her gaze every time she looked him over drove him wild, but there was nothing he could do about it.

Wickedly creative, indeed.

But he'd get his revenge. Sooner or later.

Sooner, he found, as they sat next to each other on a sofa to watch a movie. It had taken a while for the boys to agree on a film, but now they sprawled on their stomachs on the carpet, chins propped in fists. Which meant there was no one to pay attention to Gabe when he laid his arm along the back of the couch and teased the tiny curls at the back Anne's neck. He stroked her soft skin, sliding across her nape in slow sweeps. She shivered, goose bumps breaking over her arms, and he would swear he could see the outline of her nipples.

Ah, nice. He loved how quickly she responded for him.

"*What* are you doing?" she hissed.

He pitched his voice low enough that the boys wouldn't be able to hear over the volume of the movie. "Shouldn't that have been my question when you stole my shirt and then ogled me?"

"Stealing something was part of the game." Her golden eyes went wide and innocent.

He gave her a skeptical glance. "And the ogling?"

"You're welcome." Her smile was so sunny and sweet he had to smother a chortle.

He scooted a little closer, so their sides were plastered together from chest to knee. A slow burn of lust kindled in his gut. Teasing her meant teasing himself, and having her near felt far too good. But the proximity gave him a longer reach for toying with her. He slipped his fingers down the side of her throat and skimmed along her collarbone. Her breath caught and her hand came down on his knee, tension running through her body.

When he traced the neckline of her T-shirt down to its low vee, she pinched his thigh. Hard. He winced and pulled his hand back to the top of the couch, but then tugged on her hair in retribution. Not enough to hurt, but enough to make her shoot him a dirty look. Then something calculating flashed across her expression and her smile was enough to send any sane man running. Apparently, he wasn't sane because he stayed right where he was. The hand on his knee shifted inward, and her nail ran along his inseam, getting dangerously close to his shaft before her fingers danced in patterns on his thigh.

Sweat broke along his hairline, and his erection was a rigid bar in his pants within moments. He swallowed, reviewing computer programming language in his head to distract himself from what she was doing. It did nothing to cool his ardor. Finally, he grabbed her wrist and shuddered, his erection chafing against his fly.

She leaned over and whispered in his ear, "I can hide it. You can't. I win."

Indeed. There was no evidence of her desire on display, unlike him. No need to admit defeat though. God, he loved how they challenged each other. Her take-no-prisoners attitude amused the hell out of him. He choked off a laugh, threaded his fingers through her silky locks, and hauled her forward into a quick kiss. At least, he meant it to be quick. The moment their lips met, clung, he couldn't resist a second taste. Her hands balled in his shirt, but she didn't try to push him away.

His heart pounded and he nipped at her lower lip, the tart-sweet flavor of Anne sliding over his taste buds. Her scent filled his nostrils—no perfume, just pure woman. She tilted her head, sucking his upper lip into her mouth. Every muscle in his body locked tight, and his shaft throbbed painfully. Okay, this had to stop, or he was going to forget where they were and do something really stupid, like mount her right here on the couch.

Breaking the kiss, he pulled back just enough to meet her eyes. They were both breathing hard, and her pupils were dilated with lust. Her lips were swollen and red, and he wanted her so badly it might kill him. *Why* had he volunteered for babysitting again? Another mark against his sanity.

The oldest teen had glanced back to see what they were doing. The kid grinned impishly, winked, and turned back to the film. Thank God. If it had been the youngest who'd seen that, there might have been a tween-style blushing, giggling fit.

Anne sighed and shifted to face forward, resting her head against Gabe's shoulder. That felt nice. It wasn't enough with his body screaming for sex, but he forced himself to relax into the sofa. It took a few minutes for the hot desire to stop pounding through his veins and his heart rate to settle back to normal. He tried to concentrate on the film, which was some superhero teen flick. Not his normal choice, but not too bad.

Anne turned her face into his shoulder, her breathing taking on the slow, steady rhythm of sleep. Apparently, the movie wasn't as exciting for her as it was for the boys. Or the day had taken more of a toll than he'd guessed. He curled his arm around her, cuddling her close, a mixture of concern, protectiveness, and tenderness tangling within him.

When the credits started rolling, he squeezed her gently. "Hey, sleeping beauty."

"Hmm?" Her lashes fluttered, but then her eyes snapped open and she went from dead to the world to completely awake in a split second. "The movie's over?"

"Yep. Want me to tell you how it ended?"

She grinned unabashedly, clamored to her feet, and stretched. "Nope, not interested."

Snorting, he stood and went to turn off the electronics for the night. Then they took the teens back to their parents' cabin. If they could escape quickly, Gabe was hoping he might be able to talk Anne into continuing what they'd started during the movie. The family had one of the few two-bedroom suites on board, designed for those who came with children. They had age-limits for how young a kid could be on this cruise line, since it specialized in outdoor adventures rather than onboard activities.

Bridget's husband, Mark, answered the door, looking a bit worse for the wear. His hair stood up in furrows, and stress lines bracketed his mouth. The guy had clearly had a rough day. Gabe was glad his parents—and he and Anne—had been able to make it a little easier for him. The boys filed past their father, and he hugged each of them in turn. "Go brush your teeth, okay? Then you can say good night to Mom."

The teens disappeared into the second bedroom, and Anne asked, "How's Bridget?"

"She's okay." Mark ran a hand through his hair, mussing it further.

"She just took another round of pain meds, so...groggy and not entirely coherent. They got her fixed up though. Luckily, the break was clean and set well. Her other ankle isn't even sprained, thank God."

Gabe nodded. "I'm glad to hear that. I was worried."

"Me too," Anne added.

"She's bruised from the shin down on that leg, but nothing serious. She can get around on her own with crutches, though I'm guessing she'll spend the next day or two in bed." Mark tilted his head, a wry smile curving his lips. "Then again, knowing Bridget, she'll beat me out of bed in the morning."

Anne shrugged demurely. "Girls are badass like that."

The sounds of a squabble burst from the boys' bedroom, then Bridget called out faintly to ask what was going on, and Mark winced. He looked to Anne. "I'm so sorry to ask, but would you sit with her while I get the boys settled?"

"Sure, no problem."

Gabe noted he was not invited. Not that he blamed Mark. He wouldn't want some other guy hanging around his bedroom for no reason.

Anne glanced at him, shrugging as if to say, "what can you do?"

Since he couldn't outright ask her if he was invited to her cabin later, and he had no idea how long it'd take to wrestle the kids into bed, Gabe figured his chances of getting any tonight were dwindling to nil. Cock-blocking appeared to be the theme of the evening. Ah, well. There was always tomorrow night, if Anne was game.

He offered an easy smile. "Well, I'll see you all in the morning. Have a good night."

With that, he took himself off to the cabin he shared with a brand-new crewmember. His usual roommate had taken the opportunity to spend the summer guiding in the Australian Outback with his new Aussie girlfriend, which meant Gabe was stuck with a wet behind the ears college grad. The guy was nice enough, but he worked in the kitchen and spent most of his time talking about how he wanted to be a *real* chef someday...or analyzing the hotness factor of various female crewmembers and passengers. Gabe mostly ignored him.

Maybe he could get some freelance programming in tonight. He had a new software application he was working on. It wasn't as fun as what he'd hoped to be doing, but the evening wouldn't be a total wash.

There was no one in the staff hallway, which was barer than the guest areas, the carpet less plush, the wall sconces less fancy. Anne was glad she didn't see anyone, because she'd rather not explain why she'd wandered down this hall. It had taken her over an hour to escape the rambling, slightly drugged Bridget and her never-going-to-bed kids. Then she'd run into Gabe's parents getting ice once she'd left the cabin. After Anne offered a quick rundown of the evening, Peggy had given her a speculative glance and told her which room was Gabe's. Then the older woman had grinned, shot Anne a little wink, and grabbed Vince to drag him off to bed. Anne had debated all of thirty seconds before she went in search of Gabe. She wasn't sleepy anyway after her nap during the movie, so she was hoping he was as wide-awake as she was. Maybe they could wear each other out.

She knocked on his door and waited. Only a few seconds passed before it swung open. She smiled. "Hey, I was think—"

It wasn't Gabe. It was some fresh college kid. His eyes lit up like it was Christmas, and his shocked delight soon turned to a leering grin.

He propped his forearm against the doorjamb and leaned toward her. "Hey, yourself."

Anne bit back a chortle. He seemed to have taken lessons on his smolder from a cartoon character. The cartoon did it better.

Okay. She cleared her throat. Nothing to do but bravado this out. She kept her tone cool and disinterested. "Sorry, I'm looking for Gabe. Which room is his?"

The kid's grin fell away and he straightened. "Oh. Yeah, this is his room. Staff members bunk in twos."

Fantastic. That wasn't the least bit awkward. "May I speak to him, please?"

"Sure." He shoveled his hair off his forehead. "Come on in."

He walked away, gestured vaguely to something inside the room, and then there was the squeak of springs as he flopped on a bed. Anne leaned in to see if Gabe really was there. She didn't think the kid was lying, but she also didn't want to stroll into some strange guy's room.

Gabe was hunched over a laptop at a miniscule desk, the cord from a pair of earbuds trailing down his chest. She could hear the faint pounding of rock music. Well, that explained why he hadn't heard her talking to his roommate. He was intently focused on whatever he was doing, which seemed to involve a bunch of numbers and symbols scrolling by rapidly on his screen. He typed a few things, and then more symbols flew by. She stepped up behind him and tugged a short curl at the nape of his hair. If the kid had left, she might have tried a more lascivious way to get Gabe's attention, but they weren't alone.

He jolted, yanked the earbuds out, and twisted to look back. "Anne."

"Gabe."

He blinked, his eyes bloodshot. From tiredness or staring at the computer screen? He shook his head. "What are you doing here?"

Well, that was a less than enthusiastic greeting. She felt like an idiot for having come. Something constricted in her chest, and she felt a dart of pain. Heat rushed to her cheeks, and she spun for the door. "I honestly don't know."

She got maybe two steps down the hall when his hand closed around her arm and pulled her back around.

"Hey, wait. Where are you going?" His palms lifted to cup her face. "What's wrong?"

"Not a thing." She could fight his hold and try to escape, but the drama would just prolong the experience. At this point, she wanted to leave as quickly and *quietly* as possible. She pinned her gaze to his collarbone. "I just thought you'd be happier to see me. I didn't mean to interrupt...whatever you were doing."

"Coding." His thumbs stroked over her cheekbones, and a little spark sizzled through her. Annoying, at the moment. He gave her a lopsided smile. "Sorry, when I immerse myself in it, it's hard to come back to the real world. You surprised me. I didn't mean to make you feel unwelcome."

"Your roomie tried to make me feel very welcome." Because that little surprise hadn't made this any more fun. Then again, maybe she should have figured out that staff shared rooms. Most of the passengers did. And she felt like an even bigger idiot for not thinking this through.

"What did he say?" His expression darkened.

She shrugged. "Nothing inappropriate, just practiced his leer on me."

A little growl erupted from him, but then he snorted. "I'd offer to kick his ass, but let's be honest, if he needed a beating, you're more than capable of delivering it."

Well, at least one of them wasn't an idiot. She managed a small grin. "True."

Examining her face for God knew what, he finally asked, "Want to go for a walk on deck?"

Hesitating for a moment, she twisted her lips together. She should just call it a wash and head for bed. Reading a book or uploading some photos for her sisters and friends would have been a lot gentler on her ego.

"Please?" He leaned his forehead against hers, his green gaze beseeching. "Don't leave."

Wow, he was good at the pleading. And having his body heat surrounding her made her belly quiver. "Okay. I guess I could do a walk."

His smile was brilliant. "Great. Give me two seconds to grab a jacket and save what I was working on."

"Fine. I'll meet you on deck." This had already been awkward enough, so she had no desire to stand there and be gawked at or questioned by any staff who walked by. Plus, the leering roomie wasn't someone she felt the need to revisit. She slipped away and jogged up the stairs.

A chill breeze ruffled her hair and flattened her pullover against her chest as soon as she made it outside. Propping her elbows on the railing, she watched the dark water below swirl around the boat and waited for him.

Strong arms wrapped around her from behind, the scent of Gabe infused the air, and his warmth enveloped her. "Sorry about that. Again."

"No problem." Because it shouldn't matter that he hadn't been excited to see her. They'd had one session of shagging and a little petting and cuddling. That was all. It wasn't a commitment for more. She had no reason to be upset or hurt. She *wasn't* upset. Or hurt. At all. Of course not.

He brushed his lips over her nape. "God, you smell good. You feel good. I'm glad you came to my room. I didn't know when you'd be done with Bridget, if you were still tired since you crashed during the movie, or if you even wanted to see me again today. So I decided to keep myself busy, but I've never had a more welcome interruption."

Well, that was nice. A bit of balm to the pride. Not that she needed it, because she did *not*. If they continued to sleep together during this trip, there were no emotional strings attached. She'd managed affairs like that before. Sometimes you just needed some play without a relationship on top of it. With her mother and sisters as part of her package deal—and several men who'd run screaming from them—she hadn't always wanted anything other than a little sexual stress relief from a guy. Hooking up on a cruise could only be about sex. That heart-constricting ache in her chest couldn't happen again. Ever.

She cleared her throat. "What were you coding?"

"Software." He nuzzled into the side of her throat. "I do a bit of programming on the side. It's what I used to do before."

"You quit being a programmer to become a guide?" That was a surprise, even though she'd seen him coding with her own eyes.

"Yep." He nipped at her earlobe, and warmth poured through her, making her toes curl. His voice rumbled in her ear. "Got tired of the workaholic lifestyle."

"Ah." So he'd left a stable job to become an outdoor vagabond. It wasn't because he'd had no other options. He didn't *want* to have a normal profession. Yeah, there really was no chance for more than sex between them. He was a male version of her mother. She stiffened as that truth slapped her in the face like a wave of frigid seawater, though it did little to cool her ardor.

"You don't like my choice of profession, do you?" He paused, leaning back a bit, but not letting her go.

She shrugged. "Your life choices have nothing to do with me, Warren. I'm just a passenger along on this cruise, nothing more."

He was silent for a long moment. "So I shouldn't ask for your number?"

A laugh straggled out of her. She felt like a complete dolt for the way her heart skipped a beat. He hadn't meant anything by it—it was just a joke. She infused a note of teasing into her tone. "You're into sexting, huh?"

"With you? I think I'd be in to just about everything." The words were dead serious, and she didn't quite know what to make of that.

"Everything, really?" She kept her voice light. "Should we talk about that whole *Fifty Shades* thing again?"

"You want to spank me?" His arms tightened around her waist, pulling her back into his hips. She felt the thick length of him, and the warmth within her burned to something hotter and far more dangerous. Her nipples peaked and it had nothing to do with the chill breeze and everything to do with desire. Her hands moved back to grip the outsides of his muscular thighs, and she rubbed herself into his erection, making him groan softly.

She grinned at the power that rushed through her. God, but she wanted his hands on her skin. "At this point, I wouldn't mind some good old-fashioned, full-penetration missionary."

Another low groan. "Yes, please."

She glanced back. He offered up the kind of smoldering look his roommate could only dream of. It made her knees weaken and lust sluice through her.

"Tell me you grabbed condoms when you went to get your jacket."

He offered her that pirate's smile. "How about I let you strip-search me, and if I *don't* have any, you can spank me for it."

Sounded good to her. "You're on."

CHAPTER FIVE

Since Gabe had to go to some kind of staff meeting, Anne was on her own the next morning, and she decided to indulge in the rare luxury of sleeping in. Mellowness steeped through her, and she felt deliciously boneless, so she rolled over and passed back out after he left. She was only just starting to surface from slumber when her cell phone rang. Groaning, she grabbed it and pushed the answer button. "Yeah?"

The word emerged a low croak, and she had to clear her throat twice.

Meg's voice came through the line, concern coloring her tone. "Are you okay? You sound sick."

"Gee, thanks," Anne replied drily. "I was just grabbing an extra hour or two of sleep. I'm not ill."

That didn't alleviate Meg's concern. If anything, she sounded more worried. "You *never* sleep in."

True, but Anne had gotten less sleep the night before than normal. Because Gabe had brought several condoms with him and, of course, they just had to use them. She didn't really feel the need to advertise that to anyone though. Not even one of her best friends. "I'm on vacation. I can sleep in if I want to."

"Uh-huh." Meg's tone made it clear she was unconvinced, but she changed the subject anyway. "I was calling to ask how things are going. Are you getting your adrenaline on whenever you're out of bed?"

Heh. Anne had been getting her adrenaline on when she was *in* bed, actually. Sitting up, she leaned back against the headboard. "It's going well, aside from the spectacular fall of a lady who was hiking through a cave with me yesterday. She broke one leg and bruised the hell out of the other one."

"Ouch." Meg tsked sympathetically. "That's the kind of adventure you don't want."

"Exactly. How's the wedding prep?"

"Everything's fine, actually. Finn's here with me making wedding favors." His tortured moan came through the line. A wry note entered Meg's voice. "I haven't gone bridezilla even once. Though Karen's going to need her maid of honor gown let out a bit. I swear the kid likes to do handstands against her bellybutton."

"The belly alien is rebelling against his confinement." Anne made a creepy cooing sound, and her friend laughed, as expected.

"That one is going to hit the ground running."

She cracked her knuckles. "Ah, babysitting duties are gonna be so much fun."

"Right? I'm going to be an awesome auntie, though." Meg was an only child, so she'd done a lot of babysitting and auntie duties for Anne's sisters over the years. She really did have amazing friends. Without them, she might never have managed to finish college, or survived into her thirties with her sanity *mostly* intact.

"I know you will, Aunt Meg. No kid could ask for better." Anne tossed back the covers and hopped out of bed. No time like the present to get ready for the day. If she hurried, she might actually make the last few minutes of breakfast service in the dining room. She could shower after she came back.

Meg hummed. "You've already had plenty of experience with the ones who hit the ground running, what with your little sisters."

"They aren't so little anymore, thank God." She stepped into the bathroom and grabbed her toothbrush. "I'm going to get ready in your ear, just so you know."

"No problem. It's not like I haven't seen you brush your teeth and hair before. Or seen you shower in a million high school gym classes. Not that I looked too closely, but still." Meg paused for a moment. "Do you think you'll ever want kids like Karen? Or did raising your sisters burn you out?"

An image of a little girl with Gabe's green eyes and her red hair flashed through Anne's mind, and she choked on the toothpaste. *Whoa*. That was weird. And needed to never, ever happen again. There would be no breeding with Gabe unless they had a birth control malfunction. Period. End of story. She rinsed her mouth to give herself time to come up with a normal response. "No, I'm not burned out. So...maybe I'd have some of my own. If I find the right guy. I know Karen was willing to do the sperm bank thing before she reconciled with Tate, but I've already done single-parenting. That part, I don't want to do again if I don't have to."

"Fair enough." Then Meg muttered, "Since your mom was like having a fourth child to raise."

"Truer words, my friend, have never been spoken." Anne ran a brush through her sex-mussed hair. It didn't lay quite right, but oh well. It was just for breakfast. "I got to be the responsible sister-parent for years, so it's going to be fun to play auntie. Noisy toys and candy, here we come."

"You're evil."

Anne bounced into the bedroom and yanked on some clean clothes. "Yes, thank you. It's so nice to have my efforts recognized."

"I'm glad I can be there for you." There was a short pause. "So...other than rescuing fall victims, what's going on there? How did they wear you out to the point that you needed to sleep in? Did you hook up with a hot guy and have wild all-night-long sex or something?"

Anne froze. For perhaps the first time in her life, she didn't want to tell her best friends everything. She didn't even know why, but something in her chest felt odd and quivery and far too vulnerable to discuss yet. Which was just weird, since this was an affair with even fewer strings attached than normal. Gabe was an onboard fuck-buddy, nothing more. She should be singing his sexy praises to the sky, regaling her friends with tales of their exploits.

She didn't want to.

Licking her suddenly dry lips, she grabbed her room key card and said quickly, "You know, I should go. I'm going to miss the last of the breakfast service."

Meg sputtered. "Don't you dare hang up on me! You're on a cell phone. Carry me with you."

Damn, she had Anne there. "I can't take you with me and tell you what you want to know. There are children on this cruise. Probably in the dining room too."

"So, a quick recap," Meg put in briskly. "You *did* hook up with an all-nighter hottie sexfest, but you don't want to tell me about it. Am I correctly reading between those lines?"

"Um...well...yeah." Wow, that was eloquent. Anne cringed at her own banality, heat rushing up her cheeks.

"Oh my God. I can practically hear you blushing. Anne Elizabeth

Kirby is *blushing*."

She heard Finn speak in the background. "You can hear a blush? Women and their psychic powers are weird. And so are wedding favors."

"Oh, hush, and keep tying ribbons around the bubble containers. I don't want people throwing bird seed at me and you can't do rice anymore because it kills birds." The phone rustled. "Okay, I'm back, Anne. Who is he? What does he do for a living? Why *don't* you want to talk about it? Was it bad?"

Finn made an exclamation of dismay that echoed through the connection. "Gah! I'm going for a run. I'm very sure I don't want this information."

Anne heard Finn pop a loud kiss on Meg's cheek.

"Bye, honey." Meg's voice went all soft and loving, and Anne felt a kick of jealousy. She pushed it away, as usual. The wedding with all three of her besties cooing and dancing with their men was going to make moments like this stretch into a day-long spiral of envy. It was enough to make her reconsider her no-dates-at-weddings policy. Then again, there were no men back in Half Moon Bay she'd want to take with her. Gabe's face flashed before her eyes and she pushed that away too. No. Even if she was insane enough to want to take their affair home with her, he was working on the ship all summer. He'd be off on another cruise the day after she left.

"Anne!" Meg yanked her back to the present. "I need details, woman. Quit holding out on me."

"Uh...Gabe Warren. Outdoor guide for the cruise line. No, it wasn't bad." It was the best sex of her life, but confessing that felt like a really stupid idea. There was no way to take back those words when she put the idea out there. Keep it to herself and it might go away.

Yeah, that sounded pathetic and illogical even in her own head, but she went with it anyway.

"Wait." Meg turned dubious. "It was good but you don't want to talk about it. *You.*"

Jesus, it wasn't like she told her friends every move she made in bed. She wasn't closemouthed about it, but she didn't blab all the dirty details. Protesting would just make Meg more suspicious, so Anne went on the offensive instead. "Who are you and what have you done with shy Meg?"

Her friend fired back, "Shy Meg got a sex life, mostly because you strong-armed me into that trip to Vegas where I hooked up with Finn. You created a monster and now you have to live with the consequences."

And Meg scored another point in this match. Anne shifted from foot to foot, hunching her shoulders. "It was nice. Really, really mind-blowingly awesome."

"Ooooooh."

Enough already. "Stop that."

Jogging out of her cabin and down the hall meant Anne could make her way to the dining room as quickly as possible. But the extra speed didn't save her from her friend's maniacal giggling.

"It was good enough to make *you* blush, Anne. You! That must be a whole new level of orgasmic."

It had been, but she wasn't ready to tell anyone that just yet. Not even her best friends. Maybe especially not her best friends—and that was so out of character, she felt like she was having an out of body experience. No wonder Meg was confused. Anne managed a light tone. "I'm almost to breakfast, hon. I really should go."

"Uh huh. I see what you just did there. This topic is not finished. Gabe Warren must be something else, whether you want to admit it or not. As *all* of your friends can tell you, it's just fine to bring your vacation romance home with you if it's worth keeping."

"Please." Anne snorted as derisively as she could. "He's a bum—though a very man candy-ish one—who couldn't keep the honest-to-God employment he had before he turned into a professional vagabond. Does this sound familiar in a drama llama way?"

That shut Meg up. At least for a moment. "I don't think you'd hook up with someone as irresponsible and flaky as your mother, not even for a fling. There's more to this than you're saying, because it's simply not like you to be so reticent." She probed with all the shrewdness of a friend who knew Anne too well. "What's the real problem here? Is it that he has the kind of outdoorsman lifestyle you'd kill for if it didn't make you irresponsible and flaky like the drama llama?"

Yes. It felt as if she'd been sucker-punched. All the air rushed out of Anne's lungs and she had to lean against the nearest wall to stay upright. "I do *not* want to be a flake like my mother. That was out of line, Meg. I can't even believe you'd say that to me. I just...I need to go now. Breakfast."

"Wait, Anne, I—"

And then, for the first time in her life, she hung up on her best friend.

The cell started ringing immediately, but she turned it off and walked into the dining room. Though the staff was already cleaning up, she managed to snag a paper cup of coffee and a remaining bagel that she quickly slathered with some cream cheese. Then she slipped out onto the deck, plopped on a lounger, and picked at her food, trying not to run the last part of her conversation with Meg through her head on an endless loop. She failed pretty miserably.

So she was pathetically grateful when Bridget hobbled up and flopped down onto the empty lounger beside her.

The other woman sighed as she propped her bulky cast on the

cushions and laid her crutches on the floor beside her. "I hear you stopped by to visit me yesterday. I don't remember any of it."

"You were pretty looped on painkillers." And not incredibly coherent, so Anne wasn't the least bit surprised.

"Still am, just a slightly lower dose." Bridget grinned cheekily, but her expression slid into sly in a split-second. "I also hear my boys threw a monkey wrench in your date night with Camper Guru."

Anne slurped her coffee, exuding as much innocence as she could. "Who said anything about dating?"

"I'm trying to be PC." The mother of three folded her hands behind her head and managed a far more credible leer than Gabe's roommate.

"PC was never my best skill." Anne shrugged and changed the subject. Who knew she'd ever be so eager not to talk about something taboo? "How's the leg?"

"What leg? I mentioned the awesome painkillers, right? I'm feeling very nice and floaty today."

"Nice." Anne chomped on her bagel. She still wasn't particularly hungry, but if her mouth was full, she couldn't be expected to talk.

Not to be deterred, Bridget took advantage of Anne eating to go right back to her favorite topic. "So, you're shagging Gabe."

Deciding it was better not beat around the bush—also not her best skill—she met the other woman's gaze squarely. "Yeah, why?"

"Look, I'm a happily married lady." She blushed. "But allow me a moment to live vicariously. Mark is the best of the best, and I adore him, but he will never reach Gabe's hotness level."

"Yes, he is every bit as good as he looks. Better, actually," Anne replied, *sotto voce*. "Any other questions?"

Bridget looked disgruntled. "Millions, none of which I'll ask out loud."

"Good girl. Now let me finish my coffee." Anne didn't want to answer questions, because then she might have to admit aloud how truly mind-blowing the experience had been.

She might also have to admit that Meg was right. Anne would love to stay on this outdoorsy, adrenaline-laden sexfest of a cruise forever.

E ven having left corporate America behind, Gabe couldn't escape meetings. A sad but simple truth. He'd been with the cruise line long enough that he was the senior guide, so he had to relay information to the other guides—most of whom were leading various activities this morning. The captain did a debrief of the accident with Bridget, reviewed their itinerary for the day, made a few announcements. Mostly housekeeping updates, nothing too big.

Which was a very good thing, since Gabe's mind wasn't as on task as it probably should have been.

First, because he was bone-tired. Yesterday had been long and fraught with stress, then he hadn't slept more than an hour total the night before. Not that he had any complaints about that part, but his eyes felt gritty and he was smothering a yawn every thirty seconds.

Oliver came up after the meeting, offering a cup of coffee. "Long night?"

"About the same number of hours as always," Gabe answered evenly, but he accepted the liquid ambrosia anyway. He was most definitely going to need it.

Everyone else filed out of the room, getting back to work, but Gabe wasn't on duty until the bird watching trip that afternoon, so he propped his feet on the empty seat in front of him.

Oliver turned a chair around and mounted it. He grunted, "Lucky bastard. You hooked up with the hot redhead."

"I'm not telling you anything," Gabe returned mildly, though if he were honest, he'd admit he felt like a lucky bastard.

Sure, he'd been a bit disappointed that Anne judged his career choices with the same harshness he'd gotten from former coworkers. He was surprised by how much it stung. He'd always firmly believed that those who minded didn't matter and those who mattered didn't mind. The ache in his chest made that a lie for the first time in five years. He wasn't certain what to make of it, but since Anne would only be part of his life for another two weeks or so, his unexpected and unwarranted feelings didn't matter much. It *couldn't* matter much, could it?

So, he was just going to relax and enjoy this for as long as he could. Anne was as amazing in bed as she was out of it. She was fun, uninhibited, and he'd done his level best to match her every second of the night. This was about having a good time, and he'd made sure they both had a damn good time.

Lucky bastard, indeed.

"You suck." Oliver shook his head. "You got the only gorgeous, single woman on this cruise."

Gabe made a scornful noise. "It's not like you were making any moves toward her."

"Only because you scooped her up the second she stepped on board." The captain stabbed his finger at Gabe's chest, though his gaze shone with wry humor.

"I can't help if my parents dragged her over and introduced her."

"Your mommy had to fix you up." Oliver tsked. "That's shameful."

Gabe shook his head, giving his friend a pitying look. "Your jealousy is so sad to see."

"Screw you, man." But Oliver couldn't keep up the pretense and laughed.

"Thanks, I don't swing that way, but your offer is touching." Rising, Gabe slapped his buddy's shoulder while Oliver tried to duck out of the way. Gabe grinned. "Speaking of my parents, I need to meet them in a few minutes."

"If they find another hot chick, have them send her my way."

"I'll be sure to pass the request along." Gabe set his empty cup on a tray for the housekeeping staff to pick up.

"Later." Oliver scratched a thumb over his bearded cheek and yawned.

That just set Gabe off and he yawned so hugely his jaw popped. He shook his head, left, and loped up the stairs to the forward deck. His father was playing ping-pong against Anne while his mother and Bridget served as sarcasm-infused cheerleaders.

Gabe dropped a kiss on Mom's cheek, patted Bridget's shoulder, and flopped onto a free lounger. "Who's winning?"

"Your father, but Anne's not really on her game this morning." Mom tapped her chin.

Bridget added casually, "Maybe she didn't sleep well. That'll throw a girl off her stride."

Yeah, as if he was stupid enough to comment on that one. Bridget's look was just a little too knowing for his comfort. Then again, so was his mom's. *Awkward.* He went with a neutral, "Mmm."

Both women gave him the kind of sideways glance that only mothers could pull off to make their children squirm. *Oooookay.* Time to extract himself from this weirdness. He hopped out of his chair. "Hey, Dad. Take a break and let me give her some real competition."

His dad huffed. "Competition? *I'm* winning, I'll have you know."

"By *one* game! And it was because the boat rocked too hard during the first set." Anne protested from her side of the table. "I want a rematch."

Dad swung his paddle in an arc. "Didn't mess with my balance, did it? Just admit I'm better."

"Never!" Anne hollered, laughter in her voice.

"A remat—"

"Save me from Mom. She's asking questions," Gabe whispered.

Looking between Gabe, Anne, and Peggy, Vince arched his eyebrows. "You know it's a temporary reprieve only. Your mother is a rabid pitbull with lockjaw when she sets her mind to something."

"And we love her for it." Gabe sighed.

Vince blinked. "Do we?"

"Dad."

"Kidding!" His father grinned.

"Give me that." Gabe jerked the ping-pong paddle from his father's hand. "Go sit in time out and think about how much you adore your wife."

"I love her so much I'll rev her up and turn her loose on you at lunch. You'll never survive." His father smirked and went over to join Bridget and Peggy.

But Gabe ignored him because he was facing Anne for the first time since he'd left her bed that morning. She did look a little drawn and tired, slight circles under her golden eyes. She offered him a challenging smile. "You're going down, Warren."

He couldn't help it. His gaze dropped to her waist and would have gone lower if his view weren't blocked by the table. He'd certainly gone down the day before. And she'd liked it.

Catching his less than subtle change in focus, she laughed softly. "Pervert."

"Proudly, yes." He stroked his clean-shaven jaw. "No red marks today?"

"Nope." She glanced over to see if their audience was watching them. Apparently not, thank God.

"Excellent."

She swung her paddle experimentally. "You know what this thing might be good for? I never did get a chance last night."

"I had protection with me." Like her, he wasn't necessarily interested in the *Fifty Shades* stuff, but if she changed her mind, he couldn't say he wouldn't be willing to give it a try.

"Such a good boy," she purred.

"If what you told me last night means anything, I'm a very good boy."

"Hours ago." She flicked dismissive fingers. "It's so hard to remember."

"I'd be happy to remind you, if you'd like." He twirled his paddle between his fingers. "Best three out of four? No rematches. Winner gets to be on top tonight."

He smiled at her and she smiled back. He had no idea which of them had the more wicked expression, but he doubted anyone looking thought this was an innocent exchange. She hefted the ping-pong ball and swatted it at him.

Let the games begin.

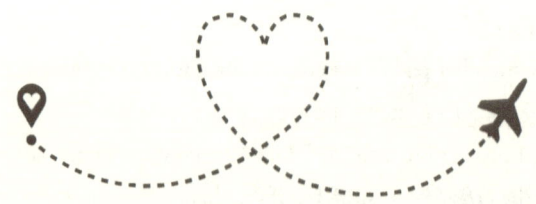

CHAPTER SIX

F rigid wind kissed Anne's cheeks as she faced a massive wall of ice that reached the height of a four-story building. Excitement pumped through her veins, fizzing like champagne. This was one of the reasons she'd picked this cruise company, because halfway through the trip, they offered an ice-climbing expedition. And here she was. A waterfall had frozen in place, tumbling over the side of a cliff in a beautiful white-blue curtain. And she was going to climb it and look down from the top of that mountain for a view that would, without a doubt, be utterly breathtaking.

She couldn't wait.

They'd scale the icy falls, hike for a few hours across the plateau at the top and then rappel down the far side, meeting up with the ship at the end of the day.

It was going to be *epic*. Anne was ready to break into song and dance, she was so thrilled. This was the kind of thing she lived for.

Remembering what Meg had said made her smile dim a little. Yes, she loved her adventures. It *didn't* mean she wanted to give up her job and security to do this full-time. There was no future in this lifestyle.

What happened when she turned fifty or sixty or seventy? Health failed eventually. This wasn't the kind of thing one did forever. Only someone as impractical as her mom would think so. In fact, Dinah's makeup consulting was far more reasonable as a job than an outdoor guide.

There was a depressing thought.

"Hey, Anne. Is this right?" Bridget's oldest son walked up, fiddling with his harness.

Gabe stood at the bottom of the ice, working with their other guide, who was climbing to the top to set the belay anchor for the rest of them.

"You have this buckle wrong." She adjusted the offending clasp for the kid, and then checked him over to make sure everything else was secured correctly. Several of the other less experienced climbers came over to ask her for help, including an older teen girl that Bridget's boy was drooling over.

The two wandered off talking, though the girl didn't seem to notice the boy was hanging on her every word.

Gabe joined Anne, bumping her shoulder with his. "Nice work. Thanks for the assist."

"Of course. I'm happy to lend a hand." It honestly hadn't occurred to her *not* to help. She was a teacher, and she had many climbing hours under her belt—combine those two and she was unlikely to keep her opinion to herself. Luckily, everyone seemed to appreciate her pitching in.

Tilting his head back, Gabe squinted at the cliff. "Should be heading up in a minute."

"How fast do you think you can climb it?"

He chuckled. "Sorry, I can't indulge your competitive side. I have to pull the ice screws on my way up so we don't leave junk behind."

"Ah, you're so smart and environmentally friendly, Camper Guru." She batted her lashes at him. He growled at her use of the nickname, and she knew if they were alone, he'd probably try to swat her backside. "What? Intelligence is one of your finest features, Guru. That, and your ass."

He smirked, turning to pull up the back of his jacket. As thick as his pants were, they still managed to cup his backside like a lover. "It *is* nice, isn't it?"

"Very." If she kept staring, she was going to start drooling worse than Bridget's kid.

"Gabe, can you look at this? Pretty please?" The teenage girl turned on her coy flirtatiousness, and her young male admirer shuffled off. Gabe put on a good-natured smile and went to see what she needed.

From the side pocket on her coat, Anne felt her phone buzz. It took her a minute to yank her glove off so she could retrieve the thing and tap the screen to view the text. It was Julie. *How come we haven't heard any more about this Gabe guy?? Meg said he rocked out with his cock out, but you've mentioned nothing in your emails. You're killing us here.*

Reception had been spotty at best on this cruise. Not surprising considering there wasn't a real city for hundreds of miles. It figured that she'd get a perfect signal *now*, when she least wanted to answer questions. She tapped in a quick reply. *I'm about to climb up a mountainside and a frozen waterfall. Turning off the phone. Love you!*

A mere split second later, Julie replied, *Wait! Is Gabe there too?*

Anne could turn off the phone and pretend she didn't get the message until later, but that wouldn't stop the harassment. It would just delay it. She sighed and answered. *Yes, why?*

Julie came back with, *I want a pic of the waterfall and Gabe! Prove he's the man candy you told Meg about.*

Snorting, Anne rolled her eyes and whipped out another text. *No,*

I am not letting you long-distance ogle.

Her friend delivered a parting shot. *Oh, please. You'd NEVER let us get away with this kind of info withholding.*

True, Anne would have insisted on all the particulars. What if her friends were tangling up with dickheads? Maybe it was because she was the oldest child, but she couldn't turn off her protective instincts. If she cared about someone, she was all up in their life and business. She couldn't help it. But she also recognized that not telling her friends anything was making them worry about her. If nothing was wrong, why was she being so secretive? That was the question she'd be asking in their place.

Honestly, she didn't know why she was being secretive. Maybe because she hadn't had anything this good is so long, she was scared if she shared it, it might disappear. Every day had brought Gabe and her a little closer. They had so many interests in common, they made each other laugh, and he could keep up with her sarcasm and not be offended when she zinged him, unlike several other men she'd dated.

But they weren't dating, were they? It was just an affair.

Maybe that was the real reason for the secretiveness—she was getting in over her head emotionally, and she was scared her friends might figure it out and caution her. She knew she needed to guard her heart better, but...damn it, she wanted to feel this *good* and not worry or need to be strong or responsible or have the whole world resting on her shoulders. Even if it was just for a little while. She wanted to be totally free, and that was how she felt with Gabe. Uninhibited. *Happy.*

Gabe came over, having extracted himself from the girl's clutches. "What's going on?"

She shrugged. "A harassing text message from one of my best friends."

"Julie, Karen, or Megan?" he asked.

Wow, he'd really been listening when she made off-hand comments about her friends. She hadn't gone into much detail about them. She wasn't sure how she felt about his attentiveness. Good, but bad because it felt good. Now that wasn't messed up, was it? "Um. It's Meg, not Megan."

"Got it." He lifted his eyebrows. "So Meg texted?"

"No, it was Julie."

"Okay." He grinned. "What's she harassing you about?"

To lie or not to lie? "Uh...you."

"Me?" His brows rose higher.

"I've mentioned you to them. Very briefly." Her lips twisted in a grin-grimace. "I said you were hot man candy. They want pictorial evidence."

"Really?" His eyes began to twinkle with evil delight.

"Plus a photo of the waterfall. I think that second request is all they're getting though." She flipped over to the camera feature on her cell and aimed it at the frozen water that seemed to be trapped mid-flow down the mountainside.

Gabe stepped into her shot. "Why don't you give them a two-for-one?"

She blinked. "You don't mind?"

"This wouldn't be my first man candy shot," he said drily.

Jealousy flashed through her, forking like vicious lightning in her chest. Lots of other women had done this, shagged Gabe on a cruise, and taken pictures home to prove they'd really managed to lay someone that hot. Which was fine, naturally. She had no problem with that. He wasn't the first man she'd ever slept with, and he wouldn't be the last. The reverse was also true. There was no reason to be upset when he mentioned she was just one in a long line of conquests.

He stared at her, then broke into a roguish smile. "Of course, most of the women taking the sexy guide photos are old ladies and soccer moms, but who am I to deny them? At least you didn't make up some pathetic excuse for why you need a picture of me for your album."

"Brutal honesty, that's me."

"One of my favorite parts about you." He glanced around quickly. No one was near them. He whispered, "That, and your ass."

A chuckle bubbled out of her. Man, he was fun. She liked that he was rarely uptight about anything. Neither was she, except when it came to her mother. And, apparently, when thinking about Gabe boinking other women. She slammed the door on that thought as quickly as possible. Nope. Not going there. Not, not, *not*.

She blew out a breath, took a couple of steps back to get a wider view on the photo, and snapped several angles. She tapped the screen to look at the images. Beautiful. Nothing could really capture the splendor of the surroundings—or of Gabe's sexiness—but the pictures were gorgeous anyway.

His arm came around her waist, a familiar weight after a more than a week of sexing it up. Unusual though, because he never got too touchy-feely while he was working. "How about a close up of us? Want me to take it? I have a longer arm."

"Sure." She handed over her phone.

"Ready?" He held it overhead, resting his cheek against her ear. "Say *man candy.*"

She couldn't help a laugh, and sang out, "Man candy!"

Bridget's kid turned from where he was taking selfies with everything from rocks and moss to ice columns trailing from the waterfall. *"What* are you guys doing?"

"I'm enjoying my vacation, kid." She winked and slipped away from Gabe. "Time to climb. Ready?"

"Heck, yeah." He grinned with shameless glee. "This is the first time

I've escaped my brothers since I got here."

"Younger siblings." She shook her head sadly. "Of course, Gabe here *is* the younger brother."

A sage look molded the teen's features. "That explains so much."

Gabe's dimples flashed, but he managed to keep a straight face. He brushed the front of his coat off, exuding all kinds of wounded dignity. "I'm going to help people who actually appreciate me. You two are beyond help."

Anne tapped a few buttons and sent the pictures of Gabe to all three of her friends. They'd share and discuss no matter what, so she might as well get it over with. She wasn't sure she wanted their critique of the photos. Gabe *was* man candy, but that wasn't all he was. He was smart, funny, and...nice. But if she said things like that to her friends, they'd assume there was more than an affair going on. That was something she would have no idea how to answer. There couldn't be more than hot sex, no matter how much she *liked* him, but tell that to her tangling, jangling emotions.

She switched off her phone and stuffed it into her jacket. No more thinking about that. She had ice climbing to do.

Gabe ran through all the procedures for how to use the tools and gear for the climb, emphasizing safety features, letting everyone practice going up a few feet while he corrected their technique. Everyone here had to have *some* climbing experience, though several had never tried ice before. Anne had taken an ice climbing skills course several years before and had done mixed mountain and ice climbing in the Sierra Nevadas. This was her third waterfall, and even then she wasn't the most skilled with ice. There was a young, über-blond couple from Denmark who'd scaled all kinds of heights, frozen and otherwise. They gravitated toward her and started chatting while others practiced. Nice kids, excellent with English, thankfully, because Anne's foreign language abilities were zilch.

With Gabe set to go last, everyone gave her sidelong glances until she volunteered to go first. Even the Danes gazed at her expectantly. *Okay, then.* This was what she got for exuding confidence and authoritativeness. She strapped on the bindings of her crampons, which added metal spikes to her boots, and stepped up to the frozen falls. Then she hooked her harness into the rope the first guide had left behind, and slipped the loops at the end of each ice tool—a small device resembling a pickaxe—around her wrists. Then she reached up and drove the tip of one tool into the ice. Lifting a foot, she stuck in the end of a metal spike. A quick boost and she was balancing on the frigid waterfall.

She fell into a smooth rhythm—right hand swinging her ice tool, left foot spiking into the frozen water, heaving her weight up, then left hand, then right foot. Her muscles ached from the strain of pulling herself upward, her breath puffed in little clouds, and it was times like this when she felt completely at peace. Her mind and body were in tune, focused on a single goal. All the bullshit in the world melted away. There was no family drama to deal with, no sibling squabbles to break up, no work politics, no outside pressure of any kind. It was just her and nature and nothing else.

The winds whipped at the bits of her hair that stuck out from under her helmet. She got about two-thirds of the way up the waterfall, swiveled at the waist, and took a good look around. The Danes were just beneath her and gaining fast, but she ignored that for a moment to just absorb it all. On the right, deep green forest and craggy rock formations spread below her; on the left, the dark blue water of Alaska's Inner Passages. Small, pale icebergs floated in the water.

It was magnificent.

Utter bliss infused her, and a huge smile curved her lips. Adrenaline and joy buzzed in her veins. The feeling was indescribable. Honestly, this was better than some of the sex she'd had. Not sex with Gabe, of course. That was in a category unto itself.

She smothered a giggle. Wilderness and great sex. What more could a girl ask for?

This was, without a doubt, the *best* vacation of all time.

D inner with his parents was a riot. After the ship had left his group on shore, it had continued on to the far side of the plateau they'd hiked, where another group had taken an easier inter- tidal shore walk. His parents had opted for the low-key walk. Appar- ently, his mother had decided to sit and rest on a boulder, only to find out it was just a particularly dirty little glacier. So she'd had to finish the trip looking like she'd had an explosive case of diarrhea. Being his mother—hey, he'd inherited his brazenness from somewhere—she'd brought the offending pants with her to show Anne and him. The way she told the story, with such offended dignity, just made it even funnier. By the end, Anne had tears rolling down her face, and Gabe's ribs ached and he could barely breathe.

"I managed not to laugh. Not even once." His father's voice rang with unqualified superiority. "I doubt you'd have pulled that off, son."

Gabe gasped, "Not even a chance."

"Oh my God." Anne squeaked between giggles. "Oh my God. *Havana omelet.* I've never heard it called that before. So disgusting!"

"My oldest boy, David, brought that home from junior high one day. Apparently, this kid had had eggs with too much hot sauce for breakfast. By the time he got to school...the situation became explo- sive. I doubt the boys invented that term, but I'm pretty sure the kid in question was called Omelet until he graduated high school." Peggy draped her filthy pants over an empty chair. "What can I say? Teen boys *are* disgusting."

"I know. I have them in my PE classes every day." Anne made a gagging noise. "They're practically feral. The thing I have to deal with most often is when they refuse to shower or wear deodorant. It's truly rank."

"Yep." Peggy stabbed a figure at Gabe. "This one *and* his brother both. I was so glad when they got their first girlfriends. They started to groom better."

Anne turned to him, sniffing the air. "Deodorant does a body good."

"There's been a couple of decades between me and my feral stage. You know I shower." It was a slightly risqué comment, since she'd *seen* him shower, but his parents didn't know that for sure.

A tiny smile curled Anne's lips, and the impish little glimmer in her gaze was just for him. He winked at her.

Of course, he caught the smug look his mother shot his father. Vince waggled his eyebrows in return. "Want to make sure *I* shower, Peggy? Or should I go feral on you?"

"Race you to the cabin." His mom hopped up, slung her pants over her arm, and grabbed a bowl of the strawberries and whipped cream that was served for dessert.

Gabe closed his eyes and stuck his fingers in his ears, imitating his teenaged self. *"Lalalala,* can't hear you. This isn't happening. Nope, nope, nope."

His mother's perfume surrounded him and then she smooched his forehead. It was muffled, but he heard her say, "Good night, dear. If genetics are good to you, you'll still be able to get it up like your dad when you're his age."

What issued from his throat was remarkably like the noise of a wounded, dying animal. He pulled his fingers away and cautiously opened his eyes. "Are they gone yet?"

Anne nodded, a mix of sympathy and unholy glee filling her expression. "Where's your trauma level? On a scale of one to ten."

"Eleven and a half," he replied drily.

"Fair enough." She waved a hand toward the buffet. "I think they have champagne to go with the strawberries. Booze helps sometimes when parents inflict this kind of torment on their children."

She sounded like she spoke from experience, but he'd found she was rather reluctant to discuss her family dynamic, and he didn't feel like playing her guru tonight. He had better things in mind. "No bubbly for me. I'd rather you distract me in other ways."

Her gaze met his, no coyness, no hesitation. She said baldly, "Come back to my room."

"Yes." He stood, tossing his napkin aside. She slung her bag over her shoulder and grabbed her bowl of strawberries and whipped cream.

At his incredulous glance, she shrugged. "What? We can't have them showing us up, can we?"

He shuddered. "I'm refusing to think about it."

"Me too, but I have no problem borrowing a good idea." She flashed him the kind of come-hither glance that he'd follow anywhere. "Let's go."

She exited the dining room with a purposeful stride that would tell no one she was headed for some naughty, full-frontal shagging. Though at this point, it was basically an open secret they were lovers. The boat wasn't that big and gossip traveled fast. Keeping anything discreet was a problem, and several passengers had seen him leaving her room early in the mornings. Anne didn't seem to mind that people knew, and he certainly didn't care what anyone thought of his sex life.

They were both single, healthy, consenting adults. There were no rules against their affair. End of discussion.

After handing him the bowl of dessert, she fished inside her bag for her cardkey. A quick swipe and they were through the door. He deposited the strawberries on the nightstand, then went into the bathroom to raid their stash of condoms. When he came back, she'd already stripped down to her underwear.

She pursed her lips. "No sense waiting. Let's get to the good part."

"I like you so much." He grinned and she wrinkled her nose, her standard expression when she was pleased but didn't want to make a big deal of it.

"Likewise, Warren. Take off your clothes."

"You first." He let his gaze trail over her appreciatively. Her skin was paler than moonlight, contrasting with her fiery hair. She unhooked her bra and snapped it toward him like a slingshot. He caught the blue scrap of cotton and let it dangle from a fingertip. Like her panties, it was sensible rather than pretty. They didn't match, which he actually liked. He'd been with women who spent way too much time worrying about that kind of crap. Anne dressed for comfort, not to impress anyone.

Her fingers caught the edge of her underwear and she pushed them down her long, slender legs. Dear God, she was lovely. It hit him every time he looked at her. Their eyes met, and it felt like a live wire sparked between them, sizzling with carnal awareness. She did it for him the way no other woman ever had before.

He already knew her pert breasts would fit perfectly in his palms. Her nipples were soft pink and puckered, ready for him to suck. The thatch of red hair between her thighs was dark with moisture, and his erection swelled with undeniable need.

"Damn," he sighed.

She knew the effect she had on him, and a siren's smile formed on her lips. "Your turn."

"My turn," he agreed.

He bent and unlaced his hiking boots, pulling them and his socks off. He straightened, unbuttoned his jeans, and shoved them and his boxers down in one movement. His shirt came last, landing in a heap on the floor with the rest of his clothes.

Her gaze was glued to his erection, and he groaned when she licked her lips. He remembered exactly what it was like to have her mouth on his shaft. So good. Everything with her was good. Even arguing was fun.

He moved over to the side of the bed and plucked a strawberry out of the bowl. He bit down, letting the juices burst over his tongue, and then chewed slowly. Her gaze locked on his lips and she swayed toward him. Her pupils expanded until only a thin ring of gold remained, and her breasts rose and fell in quick pants.

He held out the strawberry. "Want some?"

She nodded mutely and came toward him, her body a testimony to willowy grace. He lifted the fruit to her lips, and she took a bite, closing her eyes. He took shameless advantage and curved his hand over a bare breast. Her breath caught as he circled his thumb around the beaded tip. After setting the strawberry stem down, he swiped his fingers through the whipped cream, and dabbed it onto her nipple. Then he bent to lick and suck, her flavor mixing with the sugary sweetness.

Her hands clenched in his hair, her torso arching into him. She gasped, "More."

Yes. More. That always seemed to be what he wanted when she was near. *More.* He graced the other breast with cream and repeated the process, scraping over her nipple with his teeth. She moaned, rising onto her tiptoes. He kept teasing the puckered tip, flicking it with his tongue.

"My turn." She pushed at his shoulders until he eased away.

She picked up a strawberry, bit the end, and then smeared it over his nipple. The cool juices contrasted sharply with the heat pumping through his body.

She picked up the bowl and took it with her when she dropped onto the bed and settled on her back. "You know, I've always wondered what it would be like to have someone drink champagne from my belly button. Fruit juice would work just as well. Want to try it?"

He could only nod, because his tongue had stuck to the roof of his mouth. Having her laid out like a buffet before him while she suggested carnal acts was enough to make his brain short-circuit.

They experimented with licking and sucking whipped cream and strawberry juice off various body parts, every second ratcheting the tension higher, making him throb with need. When he couldn't take it anymore, he shoved the bowl back onto the nightstand, covered himself in a condom, and rolled on top of her.

"Finally." She clung to him, wrapping her arms and legs around him.

He laughed. "If you wanted me to get to the main event faster, that's all you had to say."

"I was having too much fun to stop. But now I want..." Her hips lifted in blatant offering and the shreds of his control snapped.

"Hell, yes." He slammed his length deep in one swift plunge. Her sex closed around him, so sleek and tight he had to clench his teeth to keep from coming then and there. They'd spent enough time revving each other up that he knew it wouldn't take long to shatter.

"Hurry, Gabe." Her nails dug into his back, and she undulated beneath him. He gave her what she wanted, what they both wanted. He shoved into her again and again, their skin slapping together with the force of his thrusts.

She pressed upward, urging him on with gasps and moans. He moved with her, and the pace they set for each other was hot and fast and pushed them to the very edge of their endurance. Even then, she always kept up with him, always challenged him. A smile lit her face as she rocked her pelvis up to meet his plunges, her cheeks were flushed, and he could tell from the sounds she made exactly how close she was to orgasm.

A rough whimper broke from her throat. "I'm so...I need..."

"I know." He reached between them and thumbed her nub. She groaned, long and loud, her inner muscles milking his length as she came. It was more than enough to make him explode. Come jetted from him, but he kept rocking into her, loving the feel of her channel clamping down on his shaft. It was a high like he'd never known before, better than any adrenaline rush he'd had.

He dropped his forehead into the valley of her cleavage, and she cupped the back of his skull. "That was damn good, Gabe."

"You're welcome." He turned his head and kissed the smooth swell of one breast.

She laughed and lightly smacked his shoulder. "You're crushing me. Move."

They took turns taking showers, since they were sweaty, sticky, and messy. She called the maids and had the sheets changed while he cleaned up, and he could only grin, knowing how the crew would harass him. Totally worth it.

After they collapsed bonelessly in bed, he folded his hands behind his head and let out a gusty sigh. Every single muscle in his body was relaxed, and an easy grin stretched his lips. Damn, he felt good. Every time with Anne seemed to get better, and he'd never have guessed that was possible. He couldn't complain about that lovely quirk of fate.

She lay curled on her side, her backside snugged up against his hip. The soft sound of her breathing mingled with his, the only break in the mellow silence that filled the room.

"Are you awake?" he asked, pitching his voice low in case she wasn't.

She made a snuffling little noise, but then her breathing settled into the slow, deep rhythm of sleep.

After turning to his side, he fitted his front to her back and curved his arm around her waist. Something sweet and tender expanded in his chest, but he just closed his eyes and let himself drift into a place that wasn't quite alert, but wasn't quite slumber either.

He jerked back to wakefulness when her cell phone blared out a ring. Anne groaned, reached over the side of the bed to grab her bag, and fumbled for the phone. When she looked at the screen, she groaned again, though this sound was deeper and more tortured.

"Nooooo."

"What? What's wrong?" Gabe frowned, concern spurting through him.

She sighed and sat up, tapping the screen. "Hi, Mom."

He blinked. That wasn't the sort of reaction he was used to when hearing someone speak to their parents, but he already knew Anne's family was, at best, *complicated*. She scooted around to sit on the edge of the mattress, her shoulders hunched. Should he give her privacy and leave, or should he stay and offer support? He didn't know which she'd prefer, but he knew he didn't want to leave her, so he froze in place and remained silent. From where he lay, he could only see one side of her face.

He couldn't make out the words, but her mother was loud and clearly upset. After a few minutes, it became clear that her mom had plugged in one too many appliances and managed to trip the breaker to the living room and kitchen. The power was out, the lights were off, and Mommy Dearest was in a towering tizzy. Anne patiently walked her through how to get to the breaker box in the garage and flip the correct switch to set everything to rights.

Gabe was more than a little surprised that Anne's mother seemed to have no clue what a breaker box did, let alone where it was located in her own house. He was flat out shocked when the volume on the other end grew louder after the crises had passed.

"No, Mom, I'm not coming home because you don't know how to work a circuit breaker."

What sounded like sobbing came through. Anne's voice remained calm and composed. "No. You're an adult and you need to handle things like this yourself. Or you can call one of your friends who live close by. You have other solutions besides having me there to do your bidding. And calling any of the girls isn't an option either. They're working out of town this summer."

The crying stopped abruptly, which seemed pretty suspicious to Gabe, and whatever Mommy Dearest said was in a sharp, pissed off tone. Anne's jaw flexed as if she was about to grind her teeth to powder, but she kept an even tone. "Dinah, you need to put on your big girl panties now. You have the lights back on. You're fine. I am in the middle of nowhere on a cruise ship, and I won't be near an airport until the day I'm scheduled to leave. There's no way for me to come home early even if I wanted to, which I don't."

The answer was a whiny complaint, and the tone was worthy of a toddler who needed a nap. Gabe shook his head in horrified amazement at Anne's back. What fresh hell was she living in? Her mom was unreasonable enough to expect her to abandon a very expensive trip and come home over a blown breaker? If he wasn't listening to Anne's side of the conversation and hearing how deadly serious she was, he'd assume this was some kind of joke.

Anne sighed. "No, I'm not being selfish for taking a vacation, Mom. If we continue this conversation, it's going to turn into an argument. You have power, you now know where the breaker box is and how to use it if you need to in the future. You're fine. Have a good night."

Her mother kept squawking, and it sounded like she'd dissolved into tears again when Anne tapped the button to hang up.

She glanced over her shoulder at him, her face carefully blank. "I need to send a quick text. Give me a sec?"

He nodded and her fingers flew over the screen. He craned his neck a bit but could spy nothing. "Who are you texting?"

She held the phone out for him to see. "My sisters."

The message said, *Mom blew a fuse (literally and figuratively). If she calls, don't answer.*

While he was reading, responses started coming in and her phone buzzed.

The name Hazel popped up. *Got it. Thanks for the warning. Love you!*

Cami came next. *Ugh. She drives me insane. I don't pick up anyway if I can avoid it.*

Then there was Nora. *Sounds like you answered and got the brunt of the drama mama. Sorry, hon. Try to forget it and enjoy your trip.*

Anne pulled the phone back and replied.

"What did you say?"

She sighed, glancing at him again. "Just told them I loved them, then reminded them that they are busy this summer. They are under no circumstances to let her guilt them into going to stay with her."

"Wow. Your mom is..." How the hell did he say it without sounding like a jackass? Even if her mother really was as psychotic and needy as she appeared, he doubted that was something Anne wanted to hear.

He also doubted it was something she didn't already know.

She shifted around, propping her knee on the mattress. Her lips compressed and she nodded. "Yep. That pretty much says it all. She renders even the most stalwart souls *speechless.*"

Indeed. He cleared his throat. "Uh...you live with her?"

Her expression darkened. "Nope. *She* lives with *me*, not to put too fine a point on it."

Hesitating a moment, he wondered if he should just drop the subject. But he sensed this was a sore spot, sensed that maybe this was a topic she *needed* to let out. Anne was usually so open, but whenever her mother came up in conversation with his parents or him, it was like she shoved herself down into the smallest, most repressed version of herself. It was painful to see, when he adored her live-out-loud personality. "Does your mom have...health issues?"

Her gurgling laugh had an edge of hysteria to it. "Do mental health issues count?" She slashed her hand through the air. "No, that's not true. She's perfectly healthy. She's just a drama llama mama. World champion, gold medal winning drama queen."

He met her gaze squarely. "So, you let her loose in your house...why?"

"That's complicated." Her lips twisted.

Propping himself up on his elbows, he tried to project an air of casualness. "I have time."

Her sigh was a long, low, tired sound. "Cohabitating with her was for my sisters. I told you I went to college nearby so I could help my family out. Basically, my mom is just unable to handle...life...without having a daily meltdown. She doesn't have real psychological issues that I know of, she just refuses to grow up and be an adult. Unfortunately, my dad and I have enabled her for half her life. Him for my sake, me for my sisters' sake after he died."

He tilted his head. "How old are your sisters?"

She looked as if she might be grinding her teeth again. She was frustrated and trying not to be, repressing everything. Shifting around, she resettled against the headboard. "Cami, the youngest, just finished her freshman year of college."

"Cami still lives with you too?" He pushed upright so he sat next to her.

"Nope." Her tone turned brittle, no matter how hard she tried to sound teasing. "My nest is empty, except for my mom."

He bumped his foot against hers. "You don't seem happy with the situation."

"I resent it." She averted her chin, dropping the attempt at lightness. "I love my mother, don't get me wrong, but she drives me insane. I sucked it up for a decade and a half for my sisters' sake, but...Dinah is never moving out. *Never.*"

The ferocious snarl in her voice made his eyebrows arch. The relationship she had with her mother was clearly unhealthy, and it weighed on her. Then again, it sounded like her mom was unable to maintain healthy relationships. "Have you asked her to leave?"

"I've tried." Her fists balled on her thighs. "Broad hints about wanting to downsize to a smaller place now that the girls are grown and gone. Nothing sticks. It slides off her like Teflon."

"Somehow that doesn't surprise me." Not with the attitude of entitlement that had come through the phone load and clear.

"I'd love to kick her out or just...walk away forever." Her eyes closed. "I feel like an asshole just saying that. My mom can't support herself, Gabe. She's never made enough money to make ends meet, not once in my entire life. Child support from my dad was the only thing that kept her afloat while they were separated." The look she gave him was exhausted, frustrated, and helpless. "I think she had my sisters so he'd never be able to leave her again. It's not that she doesn't love them—or me—but she didn't have us for the right reasons. I don't even think she wanted kids."

Jesus. His chest ached for her. His parents had been so good to his brother and him. They'd never doubted for even a moment that they were loved and wanted, even during the inevitable fights that came with growing up and becoming an adult. He was so damn lucky. He'd always known that, but he was giving both his parents a huge hug in the morning. He only wished Anne had had parents like his. It pissed him off that anyone—even her mother—would use her. Because that was what was happening here. He could see it, even if she couldn't. "So when your dad died, she forced you into the role of parent to your siblings and caretaker to her."

"Force isn't really the right word," she said stiffly. "I volunteered and I knew what I was getting into."

Of course, she wouldn't like being cast into the role of victim. Not Anne. It didn't matter that she should never have *had* to volunteer. She knew that, but she'd had only crappy options and she'd made the one she could live with. She was, quite possibly, the strongest person he'd ever met.

Reaching out, he laced his fingers with hers. "What was your dad like?"

A smile edged up the corners of her lips. "He was awesome. I mean, he was human and made mistakes like anyone else. After all, he *did* marry Dinah. Twice. But he was a good father to his daughters. He took us to the park every weekend to play—baseball, basketball, volleyball, soccer. Didn't matter, he loved sports. He coached my little league teams. Nora's too, when she was old enough. He passed before he could do it for Hazel or Cami, but he would have."

"So you coached for Hazel and Cami."

It wasn't a question, but she answered anyway. "Yeah, I did. It only seemed fair to give them the kind of involvement I'd had. It's what Dad would have wanted."

"You were a Daddy's Girl, huh?"

"It's difficult to imagine being a Mama's Girl with Dinah for a mother. I don't think any of my sisters are Mama's Girls either. Thankfully, none of them picked up her drama llama tendencies. My sisters fight with each other like cats trapped in a burlap sack together, but even that's gotten better with age."

He brought her hand to his lips, kissing her knuckles. "I bet they take after you. Scrappy, loyal, smart, funny. They could have done a lot worse than having you to raise them."

"Shut up." Her nose crinkled and she bumped her shoulder into his. He was fairly certain her cheeks went pink in a slight blush.

Tugging her close, he wrapped an arm around her. She didn't resist, tucking her head into the crook of his neck. He brushed a kiss over her brow. "I mean it. You're an amazing woman, Anne Kirby."

"You're not so bad yourself, Gabe. It's...nice to see someone who has such a great relationship with his parents." Her voice was wistful, and it didn't take a genius to know she wished she had that kind of bond with her mother. "And you're very good at what you do—patient, competent, helpful."

He rested his chin on the crown of her head. "I like you too. I'm sorry about your mom. You deserve better."

"Thanks," she whispered. "I *needed* this vacation so bad, you know? The last year, I've felt like I'm losing my mind. Like...is this all there is to life? Is this as good as it's going to get? Doesn't busting my butt for my family for over a decade earn me a *little* personal happiness?"

"I know what you mean. I felt the same way when I was doing the

Silicon Valley tech company grind. At first, it was thrilling to dive in and put my skills to work, be creative, do important things. After a while, I just felt trapped. Like...is this all there is to life? Living for my work? Never seeing the light of day wasn't making me happy. I was busting my butt, doing what I thought I wanted, and I still wasn't happy. So I got out."

"Just like that, you walked away from all of it?"

"I still do some freelance coding."

"Right. Did your family support your career change?"

"They were hesitant at first, especially my older brother. He's a banker, married to an account." He grinned, thinking of the last quarter's profits on investments his brother and sister-in-law had reported. David really was good at what he did, especially in this crap economy. And Raquel kept meticulous books, taking care of Gabe's taxes every year. Bless her. "They look after me financially."

Anne tensed in his arms, and he realized how she'd take what he'd said.

He squeezed her. "I meant they manage my money, not that I freeload off them."

"That's good." She nodded, her hair rustling against his shoulder. "No one deserves to be freeloaded off of. You don't seem the type, but *I* don't seem the type to put up with a freeloader, do I? Appearances can be deceiving."

"True enough." He trailed his fingertips up and down her back, and she eventually drifted off into sleep, but his thoughts wouldn't stop spinning.

So much about Anne made more sense now, having witnessed the emotional manipulation of her mother. A small part of him wanted to pull a white knight and rescue her from her crappy home life. Not that Anne would appreciate the gesture, but the instinct to protect was so strong, it shook him.

He wanted to keep her. The realization wasn't as shocking as he would have expected. His subconscious had figured this out before he'd been willing to acknowledge the truth.

He'd loved every second he'd spent with her, and it was the first time he'd ever wished that a cruise would last forever. Normally, he liked the passengers, but the close quarters meant he was *really* ready for at least a few of them to go home at the end of the trip—especially on the longer three-week jaunts. Not this time. Once this trip ended, he knew she'd disappear from his life like so much smoke. That had never bothered him before the handful of times he'd taken a lover during a cruise. Both he and the lady in question knew it was short-lived and no-strings. He'd known that with Anne too, but that didn't change the feelings burning in his chest.

He just...didn't want this to end. It was too good. They fit too perfectly. Knowing the circumstances she'd be going back to did nothing to alleviate the situation. It only made him want to keep her more.

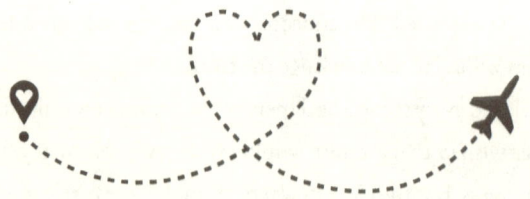

CHαPTer
seven

"**G**ood morning."

Anne's eyes weren't even open yet when she felt the warm brush of Gabe's lips over hers, and she couldn't help the smile that curved her mouth. "'Morning."

Then she remembered last night. The phone call. Her mother. Oh good Lord.

"I'm going to grab a shower." He patted her bare butt and then the mattress creaked as he rose and walked away. "You sleep a little more."

"Okay." Now she wasn't opening her eyes because she didn't want to see if he was thinking about last night too.

She was used to her mother's theatrics embarrassing the crap out of her. She'd learned to be pretty bombproof in her almost thirty-four years of life, but even then, Dinah always found ways to go the extra mile to humiliate. Whether there was anything to get excited about or not, she was going to cause a commotion. There was no *if*, only *when*.

Last night, though? Anne had wanted to crawl in a hole and die. Or fling herself overboard into the icy water. Meeting Gabe's eyes after he'd heard her mom freak the hell out over nothing had sucked. Explaining the details of her dysfunctional family had been even harder. Especially since she knew his family was so tight-knit and *nice*. She usually joked about the drama llama, laughed it off, but with Gabe sitting there looking so concerned for her, so kind and earnest, she'd confessed her desire to run away from home. Permanently.

She'd considered transferring schools so she *had* to move, but then she'd be moving away from her friends and support network for no other reason than to escape her mom. It seemed juvenile. And, in all honesty, she'd still have to have the brutal kick-out conversation because Dinah would expect to go with her. Freeloading for life.

It had to stop. That was the bottom line.

The toilet flushed, and then she heard the sink running. Gabe liked to brush his teeth before he showered; she liked to brush hers after. It was just one of those little quirks she'd noticed. Normally, she didn't pay attention to details like that. With Gabe, she seemed to want to catalog everything. Maybe so she could call it up and remember it all after they'd parted ways.

A pang hit her heart at that thought, and she shook her head at herself. The sink switched off and the shower turned on.

Maybe things being so good with Gabe was what was pushing her to finally rip free of her mother's clutches. Maybe it was seeing how functional Gabe's relationship with his parents was. Maybe it was that Vince reminded her a little of her own dad. But Anne remembered what it was like not to hate every second she spent with a parent. She remembered it wasn't *supposed* to suck this badly.

After she got home, it was time to have the come-to-Jesus talk with Dinah. Her sisters would be invading the house *en masse* for Meg's wedding, so Anne would wait until after so that her siblings weren't drawn into the fight and end up as collateral damage to the drama. The girls had grown up and moved out. It was time for Dinah to do the same, whether she liked it or not. This had been coming for a long time, and it made Anne's stomach cramp to think about it but, like her mom, it was far past time for Anne to put her big girl panties on when it came to dealing with her mom's tantrums. She didn't have to walk on eggshells anymore. There were no little sisters around to protect.

Anne also needed to tell her sisters what she intended to do, so they could brace themselves. And so they knew the Kirby family status quo was going to be shaken up a bit. Still, it had to happen. Anne sighed, and she felt like a huge weight had lifted off her shoulders. The decision was made. She just needed to go through with it. For her own sanity, she knew she would.

Her phone buzzed, vibrating itself right off the nightstand. "Crap."

She lunged for the cell, scooping it up from the carpet. The screen read *Karen*. Thank God, it wasn't her mother. She tapped the button to take the call. "Hey, hon, what's up?"

"Hang on, let me put this on speakerphone."

"Sure."

There was a slight beep, then her friend's voice sounded a little further away. "Can you hear me?"

"Loud and clear." She smiled and flopped back in bed, tucking her free hand behind her head. It was nice to hear from people who didn't want anything from her, who'd never demanded she fix their problems for them. She might have had awful luck in the mom department, but her friends rocked.

"Good," Karen said. "Okay, Julie, tell her."

Anne's interest perked up. There was news? "What? Tell me what? Julie, you just texted me yesterday afternoon. You didn't update me on any developments."

"Nothing had developed yet!" Julie protested. Then she laughed. "Lukas and I are moving in together. He asked me last night, and we went house hunting this morning. Then he went to Stanford to represent his department for the new student orientation, and I came here to meet Meg and Karen for coffee. There, you're all caught up."

The words had rushed together, but Julie's joy shone through. Anne felt a tiny pang at how all her friends were moving on with their lives, but she crushed that down. *She'd* be moving on with her life soon too, sans drama llama mama. Anne asked, "Are you staying in Half Moon Bay? Because otherwise you'll get lost."

A smattering of giggles came through the line. Julie was infamous for her lack of directional sense. She could get lost walking from the kitchen to the dining room in her own house. Okay, she wasn't quite that bad, but close.

Julie snorted. "True enough, but we're looking at a couple of places on Skyline Boulevard. A nice halfway point between HMB and the Stanford campus."

Meg piped in, "And not too many turns to get you back to HMB."

"Exactly. I found my way to the houses we saw and back all by myself." Julie sounded inordinately proud of herself.

"Ooooh, such a big girl," Anne cooed.

"Brat!" Julie retorted.

"That's awesome, though." Anne wished she were there to give her friend a hug. "I know Lukas had a rough time after his first marriage, so this is a huge step for you guys. Congrats!"

"I predict he gives her a ring by Christmas," Karen said.

"To celebrate their anniversary," Anne mused. "I could see that. Totally."

Julie shushed them. "I think we have to see if we can live together—and if I can safely navigate to and from work every day—before we start talking marriage."

"Uh huh," Karen answered, tone drier than fall leaves. "Tell Anne where he wants to take you for the holidays."

It didn't take a genius to fill in that blank. Anne grinned. "Back to Hawaii where you first met, huh? Yep, he's gonna put a ring on it. I'm with Karen on this one."

"Me too," Meg agreed. "No question."

Anne could all but hear Julie roll her eyes. "Oh, please, Meg. You just want to sprinkle your happy wedding fairy dust on people."

It was impossible to resist, really it was. Anne chuckled. "Aw, I think Meg should carry a glittery wand at her wedding. Forget the bouquet."

Meg growled. "I will spank you with my glitter wand."

"Why does everyone want to spank me lately?" The words were out of Anne's mouth before she could stop them, and she knew immediately they were a big mistake.

A round of hooting came over the phone. Julie asked coyly, "So, this Gabe likes spanking, does he?"

And she'd walked right into that one, hadn't she? Anne tucked the sheet around her and sat up in bed. "No, it's just a running gag between us."

Voice quiet, Karen pointed out, "You looked pretty happy in that picture with him, hon."

For all the mildness in her friend's tone, Anne couldn't keep the defensiveness out of hers. "He made me laugh right before he took it. He's about as sarcastic as I am, if you can believe it."

There was a long pause over the line, and Anne could almost picture her friends exchanging meaningful glances. She braced herself for whatever might be coming. The possibilities were endless, and she didn't like any of them.

Julie, ever the one to egg people on in their madness, said, "Maybe you should continue seeing him after you get home. There aren't many men with a world-class sense of sarcasm who can keep you laughing. There's something to be said for a guy who keeps you on your toes."

God, wasn't that the truth? Anne balled her fists in the covers, doing everything she could to fight off the longing that imploded within her at the idea of keeping Gabe in her life. He'd never be interested in that, especially since he'd seen for himself what a hot mess her life actually was. Plus, she wasn't sure she could handle his vagabond existence full-time. And they only had ten days left together. The time was slipping through her fingers so fast. Her throat closed with emotion, and she had to clear it before she could speak. "No, it's not like that. Besides, he travels constantly for his work. The whole long-distance thing never appealed to me."

"There's no way to compromise?" Meg words lilted with hope that Anne couldn't afford to feel.

"There you go, waving that happiness wand," Anne teased, but she sobered quickly. Because it wasn't as if she hadn't thought about what it might take to keep seeing Gabe, assuming he even wanted to. She just knew it was impossible. "Let's be real here. We just met and it's *already* time to make major concessions and compromises? If being in a relationship is that hard, there's no way it'd work."

"Relationships do take work, and there are always compromises." Karen would be the voice of experience on that one, considering how close she had come to divorce the year before. But then she sighed. "You're right, though. It shouldn't be *that* hard. It shouldn't be a huge struggle to be in a relationship. The most important question is, would the compromises it took to be in a relationship with him be worth the sacrifice?"

"I don't know. I do know I'm tired of always being the one who sacrifices. Would I eventually resent him as much as I resent my mother?"

That question was met with utter silence. Yeah, no one had a good answer for that. Anne didn't either.

"Listen, you guys. He's here and in the shower, and he's been in there long enough that he's probably—yep, the water just cut off. I should go."

Before she could hang up, Julie-the-antagonizer hurried to add, "I still think you can make it work if you want to. Don't give up on something that makes you happy. You deserve a guy who makes you laugh!"

"Have fun house hunting. Love you, guys. Bye!" And then Anne disconnected the call just as the bathroom door popped open and Gabe stuck his head out. His shaggy blond hair was mussed and sticking up from being towel dried. He still managed to be the sexiest man she'd ever laid eyes on.

He stepped into the bedroom, his muscular body like poetry in motion. "Did I hear you talking to someone?"

"Yeah, my best friends called." She drew her knees up and rested her chin on the bony plateau. She smiled and shook her head. "I got to speakerphone talk with all of them."

He sat on the edge of the mattress and tapped the tip of her nose. "That grin says something big happened. What's up?"

She liked that he could read her so well. She *shouldn't* like it, and with most other men she'd dated, she would have felt vulnerable and exposed if they could see through her so easily. Not with Gabe. Her smile widened. "One of my best friends is moving in with her boyfriend. They went house shopping today. I see wedding bells in their future."

"Hey, good for them." He squeezed her hand, looking genuinely pleased for people he didn't know. He was pleased because *she* was pleased. She liked that too.

"Yeah, he's a nice guy and he treats my girl well. As he should unless he wants me to kill him." She ignored the silent laughter that shook his shoulders. "My friends are the very best, and they deserve the best. If it wasn't for them pitching in with babysitting for my sisters, I might have lost my mind a few times over the years. They've been there for me since we were in grade school together—through Dad's death, dealing with Mom, raising my sisters. I couldn't have asked for better friends, really."

He leaned in and kissed her. "I'm glad you had them. What are they like? I've heard you mention them to my parents, but never in any great detail."

"I'm glad I had them too." She traced her fingers along his smooth jaw. He'd shaved every day since they'd started sleeping together. She wouldn't have asked it of him, but she was glad not to have to deal with constant razor burn. "They're all doing such great things with their lives now. I'm so happy for them, so proud of them. Karen's been married to Tate forever, but they hit a seriously rocky patch last year. They're well now though, about to have their first kid. I've never seen two people so thrilled by the prospect of spit-up and chronic insomnia."

He laughed. "You make parenthood sound so inviting."

She arched her eyebrows. "People assure me there are trade-offs."

"I'm sure." He tweaked her nose, and she swatted his hand away.

"Julie's the one who's moving in with her boyfriend. She owns a fiber arts store in Half Moon Bay, which she inherited from her Great-Aunt Eloise. It was pretty devastating when Eloise died. That woman was a spitfire, and regularly reduced my mother to quivering incoherency."

He snickered. "That's not nice."

"Eloise never said a word that wasn't true," Anne answered right-eously. "Frankly, I think she said the stuff my mother needed to hear. No one else ever wanted to deal with the meltdown enough to say it to Dinah's face." Wickedness danced through her and she smothered a grin. "I admit I may have deliberately thrown my mother into Eloise's path any time Dinah pissed me off too badly."

"Eloise sounds like someone I'd like, and that my mother would love."

"Oh, no doubt. Your mother has excellent taste." She chortled. There was a meeting of minds she'd *love* to witness. Too bad Eloise was gone. That old lady had been something else.

Gabe's brow puckered. "Julie runs her aunt's shop now?"

"Yep. She hooked up with a Stanford professor...a year and a half ago?" She narrowed her eyes, counting back in her head. "Maybe a little longer. They're in it for the long haul, I think."

"And the last one in your merry band? Meg-not-Megan?" He sprawled across the end of her bed and propped his head in his hand. Naked, a few stray droplets of water still clinging to his skin. He looked like every straight woman's—and gay man's—wet dream.

"Yep, then there's Meg. She's a history teacher at the same middle school I work at." She flashed a smile. "I claim credit for the fact that she's getting married at the end of the month."

"She and her fiancé had nothing to do with it?" He lifted an eye-brow, appearing skeptical and amused at the same time.

Just showed how little he knew. She sniffed. "Maybe a little, but I was the facilitator that helped Meg get out of her own way. Thus, helping her get laid regularly by a super-hot guy. I'm an awesome friend that way."

"A super-hot guy, huh?" His eyes narrowed.

"Oh, yeah. Finn is sexilicious." She gave him the most guileless expression she could manage, liking the teeny bit of jealousy that crossed his face. "He's also a good friend and a fellow gym teacher at HMB Middle School. He'd been panting after Meg since the day he was hired. Once he'd convinced me he wasn't just interested in a quick score, I graciously assisted in his romancing of my girl."

He snorted. "You're an awesome friend that way."

"I am." She laid a hand over her heart. "They fought over having me as their attendant at the wedding."

A roguish grin answered that. "Who won?"

"Well, Finn's having his dad as his best man, so I volunteered as head usher to even up the sides." She couldn't resist the urge to touch him, so she slid her foot out from under the sheet and set it against his knee. "Not that Mr. Walsh wouldn't have been happy to escort all three of Meg's besties up the aisle, but I think this works better. Meg and Finn are happy with the arrangement, and as long as they're happy, that's all that matters."

"Some super-hot guy is your date, of course." He spoke lightly, but that hint of jealousy was back, and more intense too.

Unfortunately, he had no reason to be envious. "Nah. Being the bridesmaid or usher or whatever at a wedding means you're running around trying to make sure everything runs smoothly for your friend's day. Dates tend to be a pain at times like that. Like at the hemorrhoid level. I don't need any extra pains in my ass."

He laughed hard. "Not all men are pains at weddings. Some know how to entertain themselves."

"When they don't know anyone else?" She huffed out a breath. "Unlikely. And to be fair, that's a crap situation to put someone in. This will be my eighth time as a bridesmaid or usher—yes, I've been an usher and a best woman before—and I've only taken a date to a wedding twice. The second time was only because my boyfriend was invited too."

"So he was entertained." His fingers encircled her ankle, his thumb brushing over the joint.

"More or less." She grimaced. They'd broken up a week later. "He was still an ass-pain about not having me at his side every second."

"You've been dating the wrong guys," Gabe chided. "The good ones know how to take care of themselves. You don't want a guy like your mother, who expects you to pander to every whim and be on beck and call duty 'round the clock. You deserve better."

That seemed to be everyone's line for her lately, and it was getting annoying. It wasn't like she was some pathetic doormat who let everyone walk all over her. True, she'd had to play that part occasionally in the name of domestic tranquility, but only for her mother, not for any of her lovers. She stared down her nose at Gabe. "I'm not sure if I should be complimented or insulted."

"Complimented."

"Of course you'd think so." She stuck her tongue out at him.

With lightning-quick speed, he yanked her ankle so she slid down the bed and ended up flat on her back. He was on top of her in a split-second, his green eyes intent on her mouth. "Do that again, I dare you."

She did.

They didn't come up for air again for over an hour.

F ortunately, Gabe didn't have to lead a trip until after lunch. So, the fact that Anne and he had missed the breakfast serving because they couldn't get out of bed mattered to no one except themselves. Well, his parents had teased them privately, but that was par for the course. He loved that Anne could take the ribbing without getting upset. Some of his previous girlfriends didn't care for the Warren brand of affection, but Anne gave as good as she got.

It had taken some wrangling, but he'd managed to get his parents into a couple of kayaks to join the trip he was leading now. He dipped one end of his oar into the water, then the other, propelling himself through the icy current. The wind ruffled his hair and his sleeves, but his torso was covered with a life vest. He let a breath ease out, relaxing into the familiar rhythm of his shoulders bunching as he leaned into every stroke.

They were exploring interesting rock formations and some floating icebergs today. It was an easier journey than the ice climbing and hiking, so talking his parents into it was fairly simple. Getting them into the kayaks without capsizing had been another story, but he'd managed.

They paddled side by side, laughing and chatting. He smiled, glad they were having a good time. His kayak was just behind theirs, bringing up the rear of the group, as usual.

Mark rode herd on his three boys, so when the youngest two started horsing around, he put the kibosh on it before Gabe had to say anything. Nice. He liked it when people made his job easy for him.

"This is fun," Peggy enthused, splashing way too much as she rowed. "I wouldn't want to fall in that water though. I'd freeze my ass off."

"We can't have that," Vince said gravely, an impious sparkle in his eyes.

She flashed him the kind of look that Gabe absolutely never wanted to see on his mother's face. Though he'd been seeing it often enough his entire life. His parents had never hidden their attraction to each other.

"It's amazing I didn't need more therapy as an adult," he commented to the world at large.

"Poor baby." His mother glanced back, mockery dripping from her words.

A boisterous laugh floated across the water, and he looked over to see Anne joking around with the Danish twenty-something couple who'd been on the ice climb yesterday. Outrageous didn't even begin to describe Anne, but she also drew people like a magnet. He hoped she never lost her rougher edges—it made her unique. Irresistibly so.

His mother noticed where his attention had wandered. She flicked a bit of water at him, and the droplets hit his face. She cackled. "I like her. You have my permission to marry her."

"I needed your permission?" He arched an eyebrow.

"Well, yeah." She gave him a blank stare. "Obviously."

He glanced at his dad, who just shrugged and grinned. "I like Anne too, so...enjoy. Though I'm very certain you're already doing that."

Yes, he was. No, he wasn't discussing it. Especially with his parents. His feelings for Anne were deeper and more complex than he'd ever expected them to become. He didn't know yet if that was a good thing or a bad thing—he just knew he wanted to spend as much time with her as he could. Maybe even after the cruise was over. He didn't know if she was thinking along those same lines, but she seemed to want to be in his company all the time as well. Even now, she was letting the Danish couple pull ahead of her, slowing down so the Warrens could catch up.

He glowered at his parents when they beamed. Yep, they'd noticed Anne was waiting for them too. "The two of you are insane. Did you do this to David when he met Raquel?"

"Well, yeah. Obviously." His father managed the same uncomprehending stare his mother had given.

Gabe fought the need to roll his eyes. "Big bro has a higher tolerance for pain than I ever gave him credit for."

"Have you talked to him lately?" Peggy asked slyly.

No, but he *had* exchanged emails and text messages, which were David and his preferred forms of communication. So he knew what his mother was alluding to. He gave her a saccharine smile. "You mean about how he's going to give me my first niece or nephew in about eight months?"

"You take all the fun out of surprising you." She huffed.

His grin widened, which he knew would annoy her more. "Fortunately, David got to surprise me with that. Since it was his good news and all."

She wagged a finger at him. "Don't try to be all tricky with your logic. I see right through you."

Then she squeaked and lost her grip on her paddle. It splashed in the water, and she gasped as droplets hit her. She muttered curse words under her breath, tried to reach for it, and almost overturned her kayak.

"Whoa! Stay right where you are," Gabe barked. "I will get it. Do *not* tip yourself over."

Luckily, the oar floated and he managed to maneuver his kayak around so that he could snag her paddle and hand it back to her. She looked from him to the oar, a bit of disgruntled censure in her expression. "You're not supposed to snap at your mother, Gabriel."

Dead serious, he met her gaze. "I would rather snap at you than fish you out of freezing cold water and hope you don't end up with hypothermia."

A reluctant grin quirked up one corner of her lips. "That's cheating. Undermining me with love. Bah."

He winked.

"Whoa, you almost capsized, Peggy." Anne came alongside his mother. "Are you okay?"

"I'm fine, honey." She tilted her head. "At least I'm not going to look like I peed my pants. After the Havana omelet incident, no one would believe I'm not incontinent."

"They sell Depends in the ship's gift shop if you need them, dear," Vince replied helpfully, a devilish twinkle in his gaze.

"*Why* on earth were you looking at—no." Peggy held up her hand. "No, I really don't want an answer to that. After forty years of marriage, I know better than to ask."

Anne's mouth quivered while she tried not to giggle.

Gabe looked her straight in the eyes. "All of my weirdness? I come by it honestly."

That was when she lost it entirely, hunching over as she laughed. A smile creased his face, loving the sight of her going to pieces. She was a lovely woman, but her smile made her breathtaking. A few people glanced back, smiling at them. Gabe gave them a jaunty wave, and several waved in return. His gaze swept over the kayaks, doing a quick headcount, making sure everyone was accounted for. Everything looked good. This group was large, so there were two other guides along. Still, Gabe had the most experience, so he needed to make sure everything stayed on track. The other guides nodded to him, letting him know all was well on their ends. Excellent. The one in the lead gestured to the left, indicating they would turn toward a rock outcropping that had been carved into odd shapes by centuries of ice freezes and snow run-off.

The day went by in a blur of laughter and good cheer. There was a constant flow of chatter and joking between his parents, Anne, Mark, the boys, the Danish couple, and anyone else who paddled within earshot.

More than once, his gaze met Anne's and he saw heat and awareness flash in her golden eyes. He wanted her. Now. Again. Always. He liked spending time with her, but if they'd been alone, he'd have pulled up alongside her and leaned over to steal a kiss. He couldn't do much more in a kayak, but he craved the taste of her. Since he was working, he refrained, but he *wanted*. And she knew it.

They were almost back to the ship when his dad paddled over to him. "There's a movie marathon playing on TV during dinner. Some of your mom's favorites."

"What, on one of our six channels?" It was a good thing Gabe had never been much for television, because the selection on a cruise ship was pretty limited. No sports channels, a movie station or two, and then a few of the basic broadcasting options. That was it.

"Yep. We're thinking about grabbing a tray at the beginning of the dinner service and going back to the room," Vince commented casually. "In case you had other things you wanted to do for dinner."

Great, his parents were trying to help him with his love life. That was touching, weird, and kind of pathetic all at the same time. He decided his best bet was to play dumb and mess with his father. Because that was how his family rolled. "Oh? What other things were you thinking about?"

"Smartass." Vince sniffed. "If you need me to explain it to you, you're not the son I raised."

Gabe chuckled. "Don't worry. You and Mom did a great job with the birds and bees lessons."

"Glad we could help. A well-rounded education is important." Vince nodded, a self-satisfied grin on his face.

There was no comment Gabe could make that wouldn't take the conversation in a direction he'd rather not stray. On the one hand, he was glad his parents had always been open about their love for each other. They'd been a good example of what his brother and he should be looking for in a long-term partnership. On the other hand, they were his *parents*. Enough said.

Vince sobered as the *Alaskan Adventure* loomed large before them. "You realize there's only nine days left on this trip. You're down to single digits."

"I know."

He tilted his head, his gaze probing deeper than Gabe was comfortable with. "All teasing aside, if you like her—"

"She hates my job, Dad." He sighed. "She thinks it's irresponsible."

"She's not the first. Change her mind."

"How?" It was an honest question, and he looked at his dad, hoping for some wisdom that would make the woman who fit him so well in all other areas a candidate for more than a three week mini-relationship. He honestly couldn't call it an affair or a fling anymore, not with the way he felt.

How she felt, he had no clue.

"Does she know you still do some freelance programming?"

"Yeah. She thinks leaving the security of steady employment behind was irresponsible too." He grimaced. "In all fairness, that seems to be what her mother does. Take temporary jobs and mooch off of Anne when she can't pay the bills. Her mom lives with her. Parasitizes her, I should say."

"She's scared you'd be more of the same."

"Yeah." And that hurt. He hadn't realized *how* much it stung when she'd assumed his brother's financial management was actually donations to the Feed Gabe Fund until he couldn't forget about it and the pain nagged at the back of his mind. That her assumptions hurt so much told him how serious his feelings for her were.

His dad cast him a sidelong glance. "So she doesn't know how *much* you make with your freelance work?"

"We haven't exchanged stock portfolios, no." Frustration tightened his muscles, making his paddling less smooth, so his kayak rocked in the water. "Does it matter how much is in my bank account? I wouldn't use someone I cared about like that, even if I was dead broke."

"I know." Vince's chin bobbed in a nod. "But she's been burned by someone she loves before. It's not unreasonable for her to be wary. The question is, are you prepared to overcome her fears? Is this thing you have worth the work it would take to build real trust? Think about it. If it's just sex, then have a good time. But I think you know it's not just sex. I've seen you with other girls before. You're different with her."

"I'll think about it." And that was all Gabe could say now. He needed to sort himself out, decide what he wanted with Anne, before he could talk to her about those wants.

"You do that."

Vince and Gabe were at the rear of the group, and those at the front had already started clamoring back onboard the ship. Gabe would need to help the other guides stow the kayaks, but then he was free for the evening.

A half an hour later, he managed to charm the head chef into letting him take two servings of dinner out of the dining room before they were officially open for evening service. The chef was a notorious stickler for the rules, but having been on the ship every summer for five years gave Gabe leeway most didn't enjoy. He slipped away and headed for Anne's room. After they returned from the kayak trip, they'd separated to shower in their cabins, and Gabe thought a little dinner in bed sounded like just the way to wrap up a fantastic day.

He balanced the tray on one hand and knocked with the other.

"Just a second!" Anne called.

"No problem, but your food is getting cold."

The door whipped open. "Food? What food? Gimme!"

Her stomach rumbled loudly, and she danced around him making excited little noises as he walked in and set the tray down. He laughed, turned, and dragged her into his arms. He had to kiss her. He just had to. She hummed and melted against him. Their lips met, tongues twined, and the tart-sweet flavor of her filled his mouth. Desire wound through him, an unstoppable, undeniable heat that gripped him any time she was near.

He could rarely find a private moment do this when he was on duty, and the need to hold back somehow sharpened the experience when he did get his hands on her. She still challenged him and argued with him about every damn thing, but the context had changed. Now it wasn't just to yank his chain. Half the time, it was foreplay, revving them both up for what would come later—he'd spent every single night with her since the day they'd gone to the El Capitan Cave.

Releasing her reluctantly, he licked his lips, savoring the lingering taste of her. She patted his cheek, turned, and pulled the covers off the plates. Something painful tightened in his chest just watching her. He didn't even want to think about what it was going to be like when she left and took all her sassiness and fire with her. The more he had of her—in and out of bed—the more he hated the very idea of losing her. But they'd gone into this without any intention of there being more than these few weeks. It was too late to renegotiate, wasn't it?

His dad's words echoed in his head, a reminder that everything was *different* with Anne, in the best possible way.

"Oh, you brought chocolate cake too." She clasped her hands over her heart and sighed. "You really *do* love me."

Love. The word hit him with the subtle force of a sledgehammer, and he stumbled back a step to sit down heavily on the bed. He knew she was joking. Her eyes sparkled merrily and a grin curved her lips. But for the first time in his life...maybe. The L-word didn't feel wrong. That should freak him out, but it didn't.

Dear God, he wasn't just *in lust* or *in like* or whatever other vapid term he'd used before now. He was falling for her. And that was when he did panic, because it was one thing to be in love; it was another thing to be in love alone. He was pretty damn sure he was falling and there wasn't a safety net to catch him. He usually liked a little danger to his adventures, but risking life and limb was entirely different than risking his heart.

He sucked in a steadying breath, and then startled when Anne waved a hand in front of his face.

"Earth to Gabriel."

"Yeah." He blinked, shaking himself. "Sorry."

"Wrestling with some kind of coding in your head?" She smiled and handed him a loaded plate. "That's the only other time I've seen you so zoned out of reality."

"Something like that." He was definitely wrestling with ideas in his head, just not involving code. Only he wasn't sure what to do about any of it. How would he begin to even broach that kind of topic? Normally, he was pretty open with his thoughts, but this had the potential to blow up in his face.

"You okay?" She settled beside him on the bed, concern molding her features. "Is there anything I can do to help? Do I need to give someone a beating?"

"My heroine," he teased, digging deep to find an easy tone. But that was one of the things he adored about her. She could be blunt and bitingly sarcastic, but she was also generous. From what he knew of her family and friends, she was incredibly loyal and self-sacrificing for those she loved.

Not that he wanted her to sacrifice for him, but he wouldn't mind being one of the people she loved.

Her golden gaze was earnest. "All kidding aside. If something's wrong, I'm a decent listener."

It was tempting, but he needed to wrap his head around this before he could bring it up to her. She was likely to be skittish, especially since she so clearly didn't approve of his seasonal jobs.

"I'll let you know if I need an ear." He dropped a kiss on her cheek and she wrinkled her nose with an abashed grin.

"So...are you ready to eat yet?"

He bumped her shoulder with his. "Are you threatening to steal my dinner?"

"Hell, yeah. I'm starving." She widened her eyes. "Can't you hear my stomach trying to claw its way out? It's going to try and find sustenance on its own if I don't feed it soon."

Laughing, he snagged a napkin-wrapped set of utensils off the tray. "Okay, let's eat."

"Great." She scooted back until she could lean against the head-board. Then she used the edge of her fork to cut through the cheesy lasagna. An absolutely orgasmic sound burst from her, and she gave a little shudder.

"Did you come?" He toed off his shoes, slid onto the mattress next to her, and crossed his ankles.

"It was close." She chewed slowly. "You can remind me what the real thing is like later."

"I intend to. Why do you think I'm here? The food was just a bribe to get me in the door." A lie. He loved spending time with her whether sex was on the menu or not. With all the activities available on the cruise, he noticed that she'd switched a few she'd signed up for so that she joined all the ones he was guiding. She hadn't said anything about it and neither had he, but it meant the majority of every day was spent together. They worked well as a team. Hell, with a little more experience under her belt, she could be an outdoor guide too.

Something squeezed deep within him at the thought. God, that would be amazing. Having her by his side all the time, working together for real. She'd never go for it in a million years. He already knew her well enough for that. It was a shame though. That might just be his definition of the perfect life. Anne, him, and a lifetime of adventure. He had a feeling if she was willing to admit it, if she wasn't so knee-jerk about always being the responsible one with a stable occupation, it might just be her definition of perfect too.

Too bad it would never happen.

CHAPTER EIGHT

"Ooh, look at that one!" Bridget yelped, pointing to a dolphin leaping out of the water.

They'd seen a couple of humpback whales at the beginning of their cruise, but this was an entire pod of dolphins at play. They seemed intent on putting on a good show for the humans, because they were jumping and doing somersaults at regular intervals. Passengers crowded along the rail, snapping pictures of the large aquatic mammals. Anne stood between Bridget and Gabe, with their families lined up on either side of them. Leaning forward, Anne got a fantastic shot of two dolphins flipping mid-air at the same time.

She grinned, knowing her sisters were going to love her email today. Especially Hazel, who was majoring in marine biology. "This is awesome!"

"These are Pacific white-sided dolphins. They're very social animals," Gabe said. He was the only one without a camera, but then, he probably already had a million photos of the whales and porpoises that migrated through this area of Alaska in summer.

Still, through all the fun, Anne kept hearing a death knell in her head: *two days left, two days left, two days left.* That was all she had before it was time to pack up and leave.

If she could freeze time, she would. Just crystallize it until everything stayed exactly as it was. Okay, not *exactly*, because she did miss her friends and her sisters, but she did *not* miss her mother—who'd emailed twice and called again to whine—and she didn't particularly relish the start of the school year.

Her students were fun, but there was a lot of politics and nonsense that went along with being a public school teacher. She'd mentioned that to Gabe the other day, and he'd just given her an odd look. She hadn't thought it was a huge revelation what with psychotic standardized testing, Common Core insanity, and an obesity epidemic that hit even her middle school kids. Parents wanted her to fix their child's weight problems with forty minutes of PE a day. Sadly, it took more than half-hearted exercise to eradicate an epidemic. Anne was a well-known taskmaster with her students, but her classes were as overcrowded as any other teacher's. It was hard being the person with your finger plugging the hole in the dam, knowing the whole thing was likely to crumble and bury you in the flood.

So, yeah, she was girding her loins to go back to all of it. Work, the confrontation with her mom, the wedding where all her friends were blissful and she was still alone and lonely. In her wildest dreams, Gabe would be her wedding date and he could entertain himself and not be a prick about her having to help the bride and groom that day. *Ha. Yeah, right.* Three days from now, she'd be mired in her Californian reality and he'd be sailing away on another Alaskan cruise.

She'd just...never clicked with any man the way she'd clicked with him. It was like finding the pieces to a puzzle that fit together perfectly, no twisting or shoving or forcing or trying to cut off pointy bits to make it work. That was often how she felt with guys—as if she had to squish her personality down so they didn't feel threatened, as if she needed to sand down her rough edges so she didn't rub them the wrong way. That only lasted for a short while before it just wasn't worth the effort anymore. She had to do that crap with her mom, but at least that was to protect her sisters. With men? Hell, the sex was never good enough to give herself a personality transplant.

With Gabe, she didn't have to worry about that. First, because the sex was definitely good enough; and second, because he didn't need her to repress anything. It was fucking bliss, in every possible sense of the phrase.

But she couldn't keep him because he traveled constantly, they'd never really get to be together long-term, and he had the kind of insecure employment that scared her. She knew she needed to get over all the hang ups her mom had saddled her with, but that one would be hard. Dinah's inability to secure lasting employment was what had put Anne in her current situation.

"Are you okay?" Gabe slipped his hand into hers, squeezing her fingers.

"Yeah, why?" She blinked back to the present.

"You stopped taking pictures, even when a dolphin jumped right next to the boat." He brought her hand to his lips and kissed her knuckles.

He didn't often do public displays of affection, and her heart squeezed. Leaving him behind was going to suck so bad. Somewhere in the last three weeks she'd gone and fallen in love with him. It had crept up on her and she hadn't noticed until it was way too late to protect her heart. Even if she'd seen it coming, she wasn't sure she'd have done anything to stop it. Something this sweet didn't come along very often, so it was worth the experience, even if she knew it was going to hurt in the end. Hurt was no stranger to her. The last three weeks of happiness? Yeah, that was the stranger, and she'd had a lot of fun getting to know the emotion. Now it was back to hurt.

She offered a shaky smile. "Just thinking about the cruise almost being over. I have a lot to do when I get home."

His expression clouded, none of the familiar joviality on his face. "Right. The day after tomorrow."

"Yep. We're almost done."

He flinched and said nothing.

She couldn't read his mood, which was unusual. She tightened her fingers on his. "You okay?"

"If you're done taking pictures, did you want to go back to your cabin for a little while?" He swept his thumb across the sensitive center of her palm, a dimpled smile curving his mouth.

Something wasn't quite right, but she couldn't pinpoint what. Then again, she was a little off-balance because...two days left. So maybe she was reading everything wrong. "Nobody needs you right now?"

"Not for almost an hour. We have a forest hike, remember? So if we hurry..."

"I'm game for a quickie, and I do remember the hike." She tilted her head. "Your dad reviewed the itinerary at breakfast. Like he does every morning."

He snorted. "Dad likes to stay on top of details."

"Vince cracks me up. Both of your parents do." And a tiny, treacherous part of her wished like hell she'd had a mom like Peggy. Maybe her life wouldn't be so confused and wretched right now. She certainly wouldn't have to kick Peggy out of the house.

"My parents like you too." Gabe curled an arm around her waist, steering her away from the railing.

All the passengers were so focused on the dolphin show, she doubted anyone noticed their departure. If they did, who cared? Her hours with Gabe were ticking down—she wanted to relish every moment she had left, and she didn't give a damn who knew it.

As soon as they rounded the corner and entered a hallway that would lead to her room, she grabbed his shirt and pushed him against the wall. Then she plastered herself to him, fitting her body to his familiar hard angles, especially the very interesting hardness that pressed into her belly. His arms cinched around her, and he kissed her with the same desperation that pounded through her veins. It was all lips and teeth and tongues, fighting to get closer, to press tighter.

She threaded her fingers through his hair, the rough silk of it tickling her palms. Her heart ached just thinking of never touching him again, never tasting him. He gripped her backside, shoving his thigh between hers. Then he rocked into her, the movement subtle, but it sent sparks shooting through her. The muscles of his leg flexed against her nub, and she whimpered. Her sex clenched, wetness flooding her channel.

After ripping his mouth from hers, he groaned, "Room. Immediately. Or I take you right here and now."

She laughed, nipping at his lower lip. "Well, I'm sure Bridget's kids will get the best sex-ed class of their lives when they come around that corner."

"Anne," he groaned.

The sound of voices coming up the hall made them both freeze. She whispered, "If anyone sees you, you know they'll ask you for help with something."

The whole damn crew seemed to rely on Gabe's experience and bombproof personality, and while it was nice to see how his peers respected and trusted him, it was a massive inconvenience at times like this.

"Here." He set her away from him, grabbed her arm, hustled her about ten feet down the hall, and yanked her through a doorway into a small, dark space.

She blinked to make her eyes adjust to the gloom. "What's this?"

"Storage closet." He flipped the lock, and whoever had come up behind them walked right past without pausing.

From the deep timbre, she thought it might be the captain and first mate, but she wasn't sure. And, frankly, she didn't much care. Gabe's hand was on her ass, his fingers stroking absently as he listened to their interrupters, and need shuddered through her with every stroke of his fingertips.

"Tell me you have a condom." She didn't wait for a response, just grabbed his belt and worked it open. His fly was next, and then she could slide her hand into his pants and grasp his hard shaft. His breath hissed out when she rubbed over the bulbous head, smearing the moisture there.

"Condom." He fumbled with his back pocket. "Yes, in my wallet. I learned my lesson that first time."

"Such a good Boy Scout," she purred. "Always prepared."

Chuckling, he pinched her butt with his free hand. "No more stupid nicknames."

In the dim light from under the door, she saw him yank out a foil packet and tear it open. After sliding her hand away from his erection, she let him sheath himself in latex. Anything to speed this up. And no, she absolutely felt no shame or hesitation about getting busy in a closet. Seconds counted at this point, and she was running out of them. She just wanted him, anyway, anywhere, anytime.

He spun her to face the wall. "Brace yourself."

"Just hurry." She set her palms against the smooth surface, cool on her hot flesh.

After reaching around her, he wrenched open her khakis and dipped into the front of her panties. Excitement spurted through her as he slipped into the thatch of hair at the juncture of her thighs. He stroked over her slick, sensitive flesh, pressing into her opening.

Quivers ran through her legs, a moan ripping out of her. *"Please, Gabe."*

A rumble of conversation came through the door, and both Gabe and she went rigid. She held her breath, hoping she hadn't made too much noise. She didn't want to stop. Whoever was out there paused right outside the closet, still talking.

Thirty agonizing seconds later, they moved on and air whooshed out of Anne's lungs. Gabe pulled his hand from her sex and hooked his fingers into the back of her pants, tugging her khakis and her underwear down until she was bared for him. His shaft probed at her entrance, and she tilted her hips to give him better access. He pushed in, stretching her to the limit. The angle was incredible, and she had to clench her teeth to keep from crying out. It felt so damn *good*.

He drew back and shoved in again. And again. His skin slapped against hers, the sound obscenely loud in the small room. She hissed, *"Shh."*

The last thing she wanted was someone knocking on that door, wondering what was going on in here.

He stopped thrusting and instead ground himself into her. The movement nudged the head of his shaft against her G-spot. The friction was amazing, but not...quite...enough. She reached back and gripped the outsides of his thighs, wishing he would go faster and harder, but knowing he couldn't.

Another wave of voices reached them. Apparently, the dolphins had either finished the show or lost their appeal. Damn it. She whimpered, a ragged sob breaking free.

"Shh," Gabe breathed in her ear.

"I'm trying," she whispered back. Then she had to bite her lip to keep in a moan as he pressed hard into *just* the right spot inside her. Dear God, she was going to die before this was over. But what a way to go.

He continued grinding into her, slow and maddening, ignoring the crowd that trailed by the door. She closed her eyes, excitement ratcheting higher by the moment. The forbidden aspect of what they were doing somehow made her burn even hotter. Throwing her head back against his shoulder, she dug her nails into his legs.

"This is so damn hot." His words were almost soundless, and he nipped at her earlobe.

She nodded. When he pressed his fingers into her sex again and stroked over her nub in time with the rolling of his hips. *Oh God.* Tingles broke over her skin, and she felt the first shivers of orgasm begin to build within her. The world faded to nothing and she didn't know or care if anyone else came by. Her focus turned inward, on the ecstasy and fire that roared up to claim her. Gabe's hands and hips moved faster and faster until she simply broke. Her mouth opened in a silent scream. Pleasure exploded inside her, and her sex fisted in rhythmic waves around his length.

He drew back a bit, and then shoved into her. The impact of his pelvis against her ass made her gasp, sending another wave of climax roaring through her. He was deep inside her, and it was perfect. One, two, three swift thrusts and he shuddered against her as he came. A choked groan broke from him.

They stood there, shaking and gasping for breath. His arms wrapped around her, cradling her close. She loved him so much, and it hurt so much to lose something that felt this good. What they had would wither in the real world, she *knew* that, but it didn't mean she had to like it. Tears burned the backs of her eyes, but she blinked fast to hold them at bay. She was not going to cry. She'd gone into this fully aware of how it would end, so she had no right to snivel now.

He kissed the back of her neck. "You are amazing."

Swiping at her damp eyes, she needled him, "You were louder than I was, for the record."

"We didn't get caught," he protested. Then he bit her nape. His softening shaft slipped out of her, and she heard him rustling around to clean up a bit.

Righting her pants, she zipped up. "How long do we have until we have to be at the boats for the forest hike?"

He hummed in his throat. "If we run to our respective cabins, we could hose off quickly. Want to?"

If she had the option not to walk around uncomfortably sticky, she'd take it. "Yep. Ready for me to open the door?"

He caught her elbow, reeling her in for a slow, sweet kiss. Their lips melded, tongues twining. His fingers feathered over her cheeks, his touch reverent, and moisture glutted her eyes again. She pulled back, swallowing hard.

"Okay," he said. "Now I'm ready."

She wasn't, but it didn't seem to matter. He pulled the door wide and then they went their separate ways. It felt symbolic somehow, and she hated it. Because in the very near future, they'd be separating forever.

CHAPTER NINE

This was it. In less than twelve hours, he'd lose her. They'd be docked in Juneau by morning, then the passengers would disembark and scatter to the wind. Cruise over. And he'd be alone. No more Anne. Ever. Pain seared his soul at the thought.

They walked hand in hand, taking an evening stroll on the deck. A final stroll. He didn't know if he could do this—lose her. But how could he convince her to give everything up and be as irresponsible as she thought he was? The task seemed impossible, but facing the looming end of their temporary relationship meant he had to try or regret it forever.

"Anne."

"Yes?" She swung their entwined fingers between them, though she was quieter than normal. He wasn't sure if it was because of another ugly phone call from her mother, or if it was because they'd be parting. He knew which he was hoping for.

How the hell did he broach this topic? Subtlety wasn't his strong suit. "You're leaving tomorrow."

Wow. Smooth. He cringed at his own triteness.

She cast him a sideways glance. "I'm aware."

"I'll miss you."

There, that wasn't a bad opening line. Now he just needed to keep that up and not blow this.

She seemed to freeze for a moment. Then a huge breath whooshed out of her. "I'll miss you too. I've had a great time. I knew this trip would be amazing, but you took it to the next level."

"I've had a great time too." He swallowed, nerves jangling. "I hate the idea of losing this thing we have."

Some tender emotion crossed her face, longing mixed with something he couldn't pinpoint. But hope welled inside him.

"Anne, maybe we could—"

The blaring ring of her cell phone cut him off.

She winced. "I'm sorry. I really have to take this."

Frustration strangled him as he watched her dig her phone out of her hoodie's pocket. His teeth clacked together as he shut his mouth. Damn it.

He knew her mom was supposed to pick her up from the airport tomorrow, and had bailed out an hour ago. Something about a beauty consultation. From her conversation, he learned Anne had always had one of her friends on standby as a backup plan. It saddened him that she counted on her mother *not* to come through for her. He wanted to be the one who could be there for her in the future. He wanted her by his side, but he had to make her agree with him on that point or it didn't really matter what he wanted.

"Thanks so much, Julie. You're saving my bacon." Anne heaved a sigh. "I'll see you soon! Love you too."

After she hung up, he asked, "Crisis averted?"

She made a face. "My mother is a living, breathing crisis. So, it's always best to have a Plan B, C, and D to work around her."

"Living with her can't be good for *your* mental health." He squeezed her hand. "Are you sure you want to go back to that?"

"No." She shook her head, and his heart leapt. Was she saying what he thought she was saying? But no. Of course not. She went on, "You're right, it's not good for my mental health to be locked in the same house with her. After the wedding, I'm going to quit hinting and just tell her I'm selling the house. I can do just as well in a one-bedroom condo or cottage, and she's the one piece of baggage I won't be packing up and taking with me." Her chin firmed. "These last few weeks, being around you and your parents, made it so very clear how unhealthy this has become. It has to stop. She's going to have a meltdown on a level I haven't seen since my dad filed for divorce, but I survived that, so I can survive this."

"I think that's a good decision. I wish I could be there to have your back when she blows." He met her gaze seriously. "Sometimes it helps to have an outside perspective."

"Offering to referee for me?" Her laugh gurgled out and she shook her head. "No, I can handle this. It won't be easy, but I'm strong enough to deal alone."

He had no doubts she was strong enough, but he'd hoped she might see that they were stronger together. As a team, they didn't have to carry the load alone. Life had weighed pretty heavily on her shoulders for a long time. He'd be happy to help, if she'd let him.

"I wasn't implying you couldn't deal with it alone, but maybe you shouldn't have to." He pulled her into his arms, resting his forehead against hers. "I want to keep—"

"Anne! Gabe!" Bridget and Mark came around the corner.

Another interruption. Gabe suppressed a growl. Anne stepped back, then tugged him along to meet the other couple.

Bridget gave her a quick hug. "I wanted a chance to say goodbye to you both. There's a special van coming to get us in the morning, so we don't have to hassle everyone else with my bum leg and crutching around."

Mark shook Gabe's hand, adding, "Plus, our flight's pretty early. We'd have to run to catch it if we rode with the regular passengers. No problem on a normal day, but Bridget isn't up to her normal speed."

"We wanted to thank you both for all your help the last couple of weeks." Bridget hobbled over on her crutches and hugged Gabe next. "You were both my heroes."

"Tell your boys I said goodbye." He popped a kiss on her cheek, making her grin and blush.

She glanced at Anne. "The cute one kissed me."

"Me too." Anne winked back, and Bridget giggled.

"All right, honey." Mark set a hand on his wife's back. "You've apparently had too many pain killers tonight. Time for bed."

Bridget laughed, caught his shirt, and pulled him in for a loud, juicy smooch. "I love you, Mark. You're the best hubby ever."

"That's better." He grinned, and the two turned to return the way they'd come. He glanced over his shoulder before they disappeared. "Oh, hey. I saw your parents coming this way."

"Great." Gabe waved them off, and then turned to Anne. "Want to head back to your cabin?"

Desire sparked in her gaze. "I thought you'd never ask."

He proffered his hand, and she took it. He reeled her in and dropped a soft kiss on her mouth. She suckled his lower lip, and need fisted within him. He wanted her, now and always. She rested her head on his shoulder for a moment and sighed.

"Come on." He urged her toward the stairs, the ones furthest away from where his parents had been sighted. He loved them, but he had a mission tonight, and more interruptions would not be welcome. They weren't leaving early tomorrow, so there was plenty of time left for goodbyes. However, there wasn't much time left for privacy between Anne and him.

She followed without protest, her fingers squeezing his tight. A few minutes later, they stood beside her bed, finally alone in her cabin, the door locked securely behind them.

Now to get this conversation on track.

But she planted her palms on his chest, hooked her foot behind his ankle, and shoved. He bounced against the mattress, his breath bursting out in a surprised laugh. She came down on top of him, straddling his hips. She arched into him, rubbing her sex over his through their pants. Dipping down, she nipped and sucked her way up the side of his throat until she bit his earlobe. Molten heat flowed in his veins, pumping through his body. His heart began to pound, his breathing speeding. His shaft was an iron bar, chafing against the constraints of his fly. He bracketed her waist with his hands, not sure if he wanted to bring her closer or push her away. He had plans that didn't include nudity yet. Her fingers found his nipple and twisted, and his logic short-circuited.

So much for serious discussion. It would have to wait until they were done. Hey, maybe post-coital bliss would be a better frame of mind to talk anyway.

He tugged at the bottom of her shirt, and she leaned back to let him yank the garment over her head. They wrestled each other out of their clothes, kissing and biting every inch of skin that was bared. Moans broke from their throats, sweat slicked their flesh, and shudders wracked their bodies.

Often their coupling was wild and fast and fun. This time he wanted to slow things down. He slipped his fingers into her silky hair and pulled her downward. He covered her mouth with his, licking his way between her lips. She sighed, twisted her torso back and forth, rubbing her breasts over his chest. The feel of her fired his blood the way no one else had ever managed. He loved her so damn much. She was strong and soft, smart and adventurous, funny and thoughtful, beautiful inside and out. Everything he'd ever wanted in a woman.

He stroked his palms down her back, savoring the satin warmth of her skin. If this was the last time he'd touch her, he wanted to glut himself on the experience. He wanted to remember every single second of this.

When she jerked away abruptly, he blinked. "Wha—?"

"Condom." She fumbled for his discarded pants, yanked out his wallet, and pulled out the rubber he kept there. Within seconds, she had him covered, grasped his shaft, and guided him to her entrance.

His hips arched and she pushed down, and then he was deep inside her. Her walls clamped around him, and he groaned. "Oh God."

"Wouldn't I be a god*dess?*" She flashed a jaunty smile.

"Oh goddess," he replied obediently. Then swept his hands up her back, curved his fingers over her shoulders, and slammed her down on the base of his shaft.

"Gabe!" She cried out, her knees snapping tight to his hips. Lifting and lowering herself on his length, she rode him hard. Her nails sank into his chest, and the pleasure-pain that sizzled through him made him push her faster. She kept up with him, her eyes locking with his, and he saw the rising tide of ecstasy on her expression that would soon drag them both under.

She leaned back on her hands, bracing herself on his thighs. The new angle was amazing and her channel clenched around him. Her grin made his heart cinch, and a gurgling little laugh escaped her, the sound pure joy. "I love this, Gabe."

"I love you, Anne." It took him a split second to realize she hadn't said the same thing he had, and the look of utter shock on her face told him she'd noticed the difference too.

Well, hell. If he was in for it, he might as well go *all* in.

He flipped her on her back and drove into her at exactly the speed and rhythm he knew would make her wild. He hooked his arms under her knees, drawing her legs high and wide. She moaned, her back arching. He ground his pelvis into her, giving her friction and deep penetration, the way she liked.

Her inner muscles clenched around his length, the precursor to climax. He could tell she was close to the very edge. Her gaze never left his face, and he'd swear he could see love reflected back at him. Her mouth formed his name, but no sound emerged.

He was acutely aware of all she didn't say, but the dam had broken within him, and he couldn't hold the words back. "I love you, Anne. I love you."

"I love you so much."

Every time he said it sent pleasure spiking straight to her brain. The moment was amazingly perfect, but a sob ripped out of her. Ecstasy twined with agony within her, her mind, emotions, and body all vying for dominance. He continued driving into her, and he knew exactly how to touch her, how to thrust into her to hit her G-spot. The physical won the war, a riptide that dragged her under. Incoherent sounds of rapture escaped her mouth and she moved her hips with his, racing him for climax. He forged into her again and again, seeming determined to meld them together, body and soul.

He jutted deep, the rough hair at his groin rubbing her sensitive flesh. Groaning, he shuddered with completion. *"I love you."*

"Gabe, I—" Orgasm tore through her, ripping the words away. Then there was only sensation, only the sweet, hot bliss of satisfaction. Her inner muscles milked the length of his shaft, and she rocked up into to him to push the feeling higher. She never wanted this moment to end, didn't want to face what tomorrow would bring, so she clung to the pure happiness she had in his arms. He reached between them and stroked a thumb over her nub, which set her off like a firecracker. She screamed, tingles rippling over her limbs as she bowed in a hard arc against the bed, every inch of her lighting from the inside. She simply imploded, and nothing would ever be the same again.

He collapsed to the mattress beside her, and she shivered in the aftermath of an experience she couldn't contain. It was too much, too good. She didn't even know how to react. She lay there staring at the ceiling, trying to internalize what she felt.

Nothing but the sound of their ragged breathing broke the silence in the room for long, long minutes afterward.

"You're not going to say anything, are you?" His spoke quietly, and the lack of censure in his voice made guilt shaft through her.

Swallowing, she licked her lips. "I'm not sure what to say."

His breath rushed out in a pained laugh. "I guess that says it all, doesn't it?"

She cringed, tears pooling in her eyes. "Gabe, there are a lot of reasons why we wouldn't work out as anything other than a vacation romance. Our real lives just wouldn't mesh."

After sitting up, he looked down at her. "How do you know that without even trying?"

Did he realize how much that question hurt? How much she *wanted* to try, but couldn't bear the idea of them hating each other in the end? Which would happen when she was forced to live with someone else who didn't hold a secure job, and he was forced to deal with someone who had such a huge problem with his life choices. "This was only ever supposed to be an affair. That's all!"

"Maybe that was all it was *supposed* to be, but that isn't all it is." His expression was utterly serious and sincere. "This is a relationship. You can break up with me if you want, but don't lie to yourself about what you'd be doing, about how much you'd hurt me by walking away. Or about how much it's going to hurt you to cut me out of your life."

She felt as if she'd been sucker-punched, and all she wanted to do was sob with the pain tearing through her soul. Her voice emerged a harsh whisper, "That's not fair."

"Life isn't fair. I didn't think I'd fall for you, but I did. You thought this would be easy, strings-free sex, but it isn't." He glanced away, as if he couldn't bear to look at her. "Can you honestly claim you're just going to go on your way tomorrow, whistling a merry tune, and never think of me again except as the man candy guide you scored with?"

Had other women treated him that way? Probably. She hated that he thought she was in the same shallow category. She couldn't let him believe that, even if it might be easier for both of them if she broke it off with that kind of no-going-back sharpness.

"No," she said, pushing herself upright and grabbing a pillow to cover her nudity, though she felt more stripped bare than she ever had in her life. But that was what love did sometimes, wasn't it? Stripped you defenseless and then kicked you while you were down. "I didn't...I *don't* think of you that way."

"So I do matter to you? This was more than an easy lay?" His green gaze pinned her in place, his expression so open and vulnerable that she couldn't lie to him, even if logic told her she should.

"Yes," she rasped. "This was more."

Much, much more. It just couldn't last. She had to cling to that bitter truth for all she was worth, because she wanted to dive into his arms, confess every feeling she had for him, and gamble on them working it out. But that kind of gamble wouldn't pay off.

He shifted on the bed to face her fully. "Anne."

"Yeah?"

"I'm going to lay it all out for you. You like blunt honesty, right?" He took a breath. "I think you should also quit your teaching job and become an outdoor guide. You're a natural."

A high-pitched laugh ripped out of her, and she knew it emerged a little hysterical. She laughed until she had tears in her eyes, until she had to brace her hand against the bed to keep from falling off the side. "Oh my God. Oh my God. That's funny."

"I wasn't kidding," he said stiffly.

"It was funny because one of my friends suggested the same thing." She straightened and wiped her eyes. "Seriously, knowing how my mom is, can you imagine me being able to deal with that level of uncertainty? I've lived hand to mouth, praying I was able to cover all the bills so my sisters could eat better than ramen, and I might have a drama llama style meltdown if I had to do that again. No, I'm sorry. That nuts. That's a cruel joke, not a hilarious one."

He seemed to pale under his tan, but his jaw firmed. "You hate being a teacher."

"I don't *hate* it." Yeah, she sounded far more defensive that she probably should. Which was telling, wasn't it? She hugged her pillow and curled her toes into the sheets.

"You wanted to be a forest ranger." He poked a finger at her.

Her chin rose. "Life doesn't always give you what you want."

"You hate the idea of going home." His gaze dared her to disagree, to lie to him or herself. "I can feel the dread oozing out of you, and it's gotten worse the closer we've gotten to Juneau."

Direct hit. She sucked in a breath, wincing. She clenched her fingers into the pillowcase. "That's more about dealing with my mother than my work, and you know I'm planning to sell the house and move away from her."

"I don't buy that," he stated flatly. "It's also about not wanting to go back to a job you don't love. Life is too short to live it unhappy."

"Life is too long not to have a retirement pension," she fired back.

He arched an eyebrow. "Is that your only worry?"

"Don't even go there, Camper Guru," she snapped. "My worry is founded in solid facts. I've seen how being an unreliable flake can fuck up your family. I've seen how it's a struggle to make ends meet. I do not want to be a burden on my younger sisters when I'm too old or injured to keep working. Then I'll be penniless *and* worthless. I would never do that to them or to myself."

He shook his head, looking mulish. "There are ways to be financially solvent and only have seasonal employment. It's not one or the other. If you would just—"

"Gabe, I can't have this discussion." She cut him off, because she'd heard every justification for not having a real career a person could come up with. From her mother. "I'm not giving up a good job with all the health insurance and retirement perks to run around the wilderness. It's irresponsible and just plain stupid."

"You mean *I'm* irresponsible and stupid, don't you?" He stiffened.

"No." She set her fingers on his wrist, glad he didn't pull away. She wasn't handling this well, but she was unapologetically frank. Gentle finesse was called for here, and she didn't think she or Gabe possessed the necessary skills not to eviscerate each other. Still, she tried. She loved him too much to want to hurt him. "What's right for you isn't necessarily right for me. I'm glad you're happy with your life, but I wouldn't be. Sure, I'd love the work, but I'd spend every day worrying about how it was all going to work out when something went wrong.

Because something always goes wrong. I enjoy walking on the wild side, Gabe, but I need a safety net. To be clear, that's about *me,* not about you."

"I can be your safety net." He turned his arm, catching her hand, and squeezing.

"No, you can't." Her laugh emerged closer to a sob. The problem wasn't that she didn't like his idea. The problem was that she liked it far too much. "What if we're both injured at the same time? We'll definitely both grow old at the same time. That's no way to plan for the future."

"It's not as black and white as you're painting it." He leaned forward, his gaze earnest, but something desperate also flashed in his expression.

She tugged away from his grip. "Don't tempt me with what I *know* is wrong, Gabe, what I know would make me unhappy in the end. If you care about me at all, you'll stop now."

"I more than care. I *love* you." That desperation shone more intensely. "Is it me who would make you unhappy, or just my lifestyle?"

"Can you have one without the other?" She held up her hand, stopping anything he might have said. "Don't answer that. I have to go home. I promised to be there for Meg and Finn. I'm in the wedding. And I never break promises to my friends. I've had my mom do that to me too often to do it to anyone else, especially the people I love."

"I know." He forked his fingers through the shaggy gold of his hair. A lock fell over his forehead, and she wanted to push it back, wanted to touch him so much it hurt. She kept her hands to herself.

"I'm sorry, Gabe. I never wanted to hurt you, but I don't think we're long-term relationship material." She bit her lip, willing herself not to bawl like a baby. She would not have a meltdown. She was *not* sinking down to her mother's level when she didn't get her way. But, damn, she wanted to.

She could wish that she or Gabe were a different sort of person, that their existences could mesh seamlessly, but that was a foolish wish. She didn't believe in being foolish.

He watched her for several minutes, and then an honesty more brutal than even she managed came out of his mouth. "You're making a huge mistake, and I think deep down you know it. You're hurting us both because you're too fucking scared to get over what your mom has put you through. You could have a life you actually *want*, but you're playing the gutless coward instead. That's not you, Anne. That's not the woman I love."

It would have been less painful if he'd slapped her. *Scared. Coward.* A tiny part of her mind recognized some truth in what he'd said, but she pushed that away. She needed to stay the course, no matter what. She'd looked at the situation from every angle, and there were no good choices, there was just the best of bad options.

She'd made her decision, for better or for worse.

He pushed to his feet and shoved himself back into his clothes.

"Goodbye, Anne. I hope your retirement plan makes you happy."

It took every ounce of her control not to call him back when he strode out of her room, letting the door snap shut behind him. She stared into space for hours, arguing with herself. She'd done the right thing, for him and for herself. Maybe someday he'd realize it and understand it hadn't been easy for her. But she'd never know, would she? After tomorrow, she'd never see or hear from him again.

At some point during the night, she crawled out of bed, packed her bag, and showered his scent from her body. There was no way she'd sleep, and she couldn't bear to stay in the room where so much love had been made. She bundled into a jacket and went to sit in a lounge chair on the deck, watching the sunrise. She willed the time to pass faster.

The sooner this was over, the sooner she could put him behind her.

CHapTer Ten

"I can't believe you let her get away." His mother shook her head at him. "If you don't snap her up, Gabriel, someone else will. And you'll feel like an idiot because you were too busy shoving your thumb up your butt to even ask her to stay with you."

They sat in uncomfortable chairs in the airport. His dad had gone to fetch coffee while they waited to board. His parents' flight had been delayed by several hours, so they'd decided not to go through security screening just yet. Which gave his mom ample opportunity to rub salt in Gabe's raw feelings.

Fantastic, the day just got better and better. He hadn't thought it could be worse than watching Anne disappear into the belly of a plane an hour ago. Some stupid part of him had hoped she'd turn around and come running back to him. He was a gigantic fool, and he'd stood at the window watching her flight taxi down the runway and take off.

That was it. Done. Over. She was gone. Forever.

If he thought bending over and howling like a wounded animal would mitigate even a little of his pain, he'd have tried it. But nothing was going to make this awful feeling better. Nothing.

"I mentioned the possibility of her being an outdoor guide like me and she laughed in my face."

"Oh." Some of Mom's self-righteousness deflated.

His smile was unamused. "Yeah. Oh."

"Why? She'd be great at it." She squinted at him. "Is it the money thing? Did you tell her you could keep her financially comfortable for life? Or were you a stubborn ass who expected her to give up everything, just like that?"

Since he wanted to snap obscenities and anatomically impossible suggestions, he kept his mouth shut. She was his mother, after all.

She sighed and set a palm against his jaw. "Baby, I haven't seen you this miserable since you worked for that start-up company and were chained to your desk."

Miserable. There was the perfect word to describe how he felt right now. And yes, he hadn't felt this soul-suckingly terrible since he'd lived in the Silicon Valley.

"Go after her," she urged. "She loves you. You love her. Work it out."

He shook his head, embarrassing moisture burning his eyes. "She thinks being with me would make her an irresponsible slacker."

"She's scared."

He swiped at his face, clearing his throat. "Her mother is an irresponsible slacker that Anne's let freeload off her for years, because she wanted to make sure her sisters were raised in a stable home."

"Your dad said something like that." Peggy's face was sympathetic and proud at once. "I knew she was a good girl, but I like her even better now."

Anne was the best. More amazing than any other woman he'd ever known. And she'd stomped all over his heart last night. He didn't love her any less, masochist that he was. "She's scared she'll end up like her mother."

"Poor lamb. That has to be hard." She patted his knee. "She's a tough cookie, but even the tough ones have their breaking point."

He eyed her, trying for a teasing note. "Even you?"

"Even me." She sighed, her brow knitting in a frown. "What if you didn't ask her to give up her life and security?"

"What do you mean? There's not going to be much work in her small town for a guide like me. Plus, I love what I do. *She* would love doing this too, if she'd only admit it." Yeah, there was a hint of anger and bitterness to that last part. He wasn't proud of it, but he'd lost the perfect woman because she was too stubborn to see the truth.

"So give her time to warm up to the idea." His mom shook her head. "Men. Your gender is so black-and-white, so all-or-nothing. Maybe try *compromising*. Maybe try being the first one to bend in order to make a real relationship work."

"What would that look like?" He snorted, trying to force himself to relax and failing. "Long-distance for three-quarters of the year? Is that the kind of relationship you'd want with anyone?"

Her expression held more than a little censure. "Maybe you could base yourself in Half Moon Bay, do weekend trips to the mountains, river rafting, maybe some one- or two-week trips. Both of you could do most of the summer on your cruise ships. That doesn't sound so bad, does it? Different than the life you have now, but this way neither one of you sacrifices everything for the other—which would only breed resentment."

It didn't sound bad, actually. That rankled. "I still don't think she's happy with her current job. Would she resent me anyway for doing what she wished she could?"

"Nah. Anne's not the type." His mother's grin was smug. "Within a year or two, she'll pack it up and come with you."

"I'm glad one of us is confident," he replied, tone dry.

"She loves you, honey." She squeezed his forearm. "And *you* love *her*, which is more to the point of this conversation. Love is worth fighting for, worth compromising for, especially when you love someone as awesome as her."

But did Anne love him? He thought so, but he was also painfully aware that he was the only one who'd said it. She'd just walked—no *run*—away from even the idea of their relationship. He had a feeling she was running as much from herself as from him, but what proof did he have? What hope had she left him with? None. All he had to go on were his own instincts. If he went after her the way his mother suggested, he'd be taking one hell of a risk.

He met Mom's gaze. "I'll think about it."

"Good." She leaned back in her chair. "Don't forget you have a trump card to play."

"What's that?" Because he could use a trump card right about now.

She spread her arms and gestured down at herself. "Me, dummy. And your father. Anne adores us. She might marry you just to keep us as parents. Don't discount being able to offer fabulous in-laws. Women think about these things."

"Your modesty and support is touching, Mother." He sniffled theatrically, dabbing at the corner of his eye. "Really, it brings a tear."

She swatted his shoulder, and looked as if she wanted to launch into another lecture, but Vince showed up with liquid caffeine and that kept her quiet for a while. It also gave Gabe the time to do some soul searching.

Maybe he hadn't handled the situation well. He'd known Anne would be wary, but he'd been terrified of losing her, so he'd pushed too hard and lost her anyway. Bad move.

So, how was he going to fix this? He loved her too damn much to give up now. Determination solidified within him. He might get his heart drop-kicked again, but she was worth the risk. She was worth everything. And he'd guess the misery eating away at him since she'd departed would only get worse. Time was supposed to heal all wounds, and yet when it came to living without Anne...he didn't think so.

H er mother started whining the moment Anne walked through the door. Julie had picked her up from the airport, taken one look at her, and driven her straight to Karen's place. Meg had met them there, and Anne had given them the barest bones version of what had happened. Her friends knew she wasn't telling them everything, but Anne just...couldn't open up about it. Not yet. Maybe not ever. They'd stuffed her with good food, pampered her for a few hours, offered to let her stay in each of their guest bedrooms, but Anne had refused.

So Julie had driven Anne home, and her mother was in her face before she could even say hello.

"It's about time you got here." Dinah folded her arms across her breasts, pouting. "Your flight was supposed to land hours ago. I checked online and it wasn't late. Where have you been?"

"I had dinner at Karen's. You knew Julie was picking me up, and you told me you were busy at a client's house with a makeup consultation, so there didn't seem to be a reason to rush home." Because her mother had forgotten about her, as usual. Anne was never her priority. She was used to it by now, and always had her backup plans in place.

"I was *working.*" Dinah sighed like a true martyr. "Isn't that what you're constantly nagging me to do?"

A little help with the bills didn't seem like an outrageous, nagging thing to ask for, but Anne didn't say that. She dropped her cross-body bag on the couch, walked to the laundry room at the rear of the house and shucked her backpack. Might as well start the wash immediately. It'd keep her hands occupied.

"You could have at least brought me some dinner too." Mom gave her a look that was loaded with hurt feelings and reproach.

Anne opened the top of her backpack, ignoring the look and the attempt at making her feel guilty. She'd been traveling all day, she was exhausted emotionally and physically, everything inside her *ached* and, frankly, she was not responsible for feeding her mother. Dinah was perfectly capable of cooking, microwaving, or buying take-out.

"I didn't like being here alone, Annie." Her mother's voice wobbled. "I want you to promise you'll never abandon me for that long again."

That made Anne freeze in place. She straightened and stared at her mother. She had no way of knowing exactly what her expression looked like, but her mom backed up a couple of steps.

"I will go on any trip I want, whenever I want, for as long as I want. I am an adult." Her voice was low, calm, and ice cold. "You are a full-grown woman, Dinah Kirby, and you don't need me here to take care of you. I am not at your beck and call. Do I make myself clear?"

Lips trembling, her mom laid a hand to her breast. "Why is it so *wrong* to miss my daughter?"

"You didn't say you missed me, you said you didn't like being here on your own. Those are very different things."

"What's gotten into you, Anne? You're acting so nasty and mean." More voice wobbling, more attempts at guilt. "How can you speak to me this way? I'm your mother. I sacrificed so much of my life to raise you, and here you are, being so ungrateful."

She'd sacrificed? *She'd* sacrificed? Anne's head was going to explode.

A scream of primal rage welled up in her throat, and she balled her fists, trying to choke it down. What emerged instead was even worse.

She burst into tears.

She wasn't sure who was more horrified—her or her mother. Anne wasn't the one who cried, she didn't have breakdowns. She was the one with her shit together.

"Oh, honey. What's wrong? Is it man trouble?" Because Dinah was the queen of man trouble, since she went through boyfriends even more quickly than she went through jobs. Anne had forbidden her from bringing any dates home *ever*, which was the only time she'd put her foot down about anything with her mother. Now, Anne had man trouble too. Something almost excited gleamed in Mom's gaze, but her face folded into concerned lines. "Tell me all about it. I'm sure I've been through it before."

Without a shadow of a doubt, Anne knew her mother would make this about herself. She'd seen this so many times. Whenever her sisters or she had something go wrong, Mom used it as an excuse to have a meltdown, to cry and carry on, and generally bring the attention back to her. As much as she loved her mother, Anne knew—had always known—that Dinah was a basically selfish human being. Her children had always come second, would always come second, to whatever she wanted or needed.

Anne could accept that. It was just who Dinah Kirby was. There was no changing her into someone else.

But the thought of her taking this huge gaping maw of pain inside of Anne and making it fodder for her drama was just...no. *Hell* no. What Anne had with Gabe was never, ever going to be something Dinah got to twist or manipulate for her own attention-whoring benefit.

That dried Anne's tears and turned the resentment that had built and built within her for years into something dangerously close to hate.

She couldn't do it, couldn't be here. It was like trying to squeeze herself into an outfit she'd outgrown. The seams were about to split. After zipping her backpack again, she slung it over her shoulders and headed for the front door. She snagged her bag from the sofa on the way.

Her mother scrambled behind her. "Where are you going? You can't leave. I've been here for *weeks* alone."

"You'll be fine, Mom." She shoved her pack into the trunk of her subcompact.

"I won't be fine." Two fat tears rolled down Dinah's face. "What's going on? Why are you acting like this? How can you abandon me *again?*"

Anne crawled into her car and slammed the door, shutting out the sound of her mother, who started to sob like a small, inconsolable child. She backed out of the driveway and drove aimlessly for almost an hour. She didn't cry, didn't think, just drove.

Finally, she pulled to the side of the road, dug her cell phone out of her bag, and called Julie. "Hey, do you need some help packing for your big move?"

And that was how the next week and a half went. Anne camped out with Julie for a couple of days until her sisters got into town for the wedding, and then she went back home to be with them. Dinah tried to be extra shades of nice because she no doubt sensed that she'd pushed too far this time, but Anne didn't give a damn. Frankly, she didn't really care about much of anything right now. She was just numb.

She attended the prerequisite meetings for the start of the school year, but none of the information seemed to gel in her mind. She joined her friends for all the wedding preparations, and went through the motions for their benefit. She laughed when she was supposed to laugh, smiled when she was supposed to smile, but she didn't feel any of it.

It all felt so empty. *She* felt empty.

Except when she was missing Gabe, which was always.

CHAPTER ELEVEN

S he was so beautiful. Maybe at a wedding, he should be looking at the bride, but Gabe couldn't tear his gaze away from Anne.

She wore the same floaty strapless navy dress as the bridesmaids, but she stood on the groom's side, next to the best man. They were on a bluff overlooking a gorgeous stretch of the Pacific Ocean, a breeze blew, and the weather was seventy-five and sunny. But Gabe's focus was on Anne, not the view.

God, he'd missed her. Every single second since she'd left him in Alaska had been a torment. It was an ache that wouldn't quit. It had also sucked pretty hard to realize he didn't have her phone number, email, or home address. He hadn't needed any of those things on the cruise, but he'd remembered that her friend Julie ran a fiber arts store in Half Moon Bay. It wasn't exactly a big town—how many shops like that would have an owner named Julie? So, he'd done a web search and called her friend's business. At the very least, she'd know him from the ice climbing pictures Anne had sent.

It turned out all three of her best friends had been more than willing to help him out with his campaign to get Anne back. They'd told him to forget the phone or email—he needed to show up in the one place she couldn't run away. Gabe and his entire family had received impromptu invitations to Meg's wedding. Since his mother had pointed out that his fabulous family was his trump card, he'd made damn sure all the Warrens were in attendance. His parents, brother, and sister-in-law sat beside him in a row toward the back.

Anne's sister, Hazel, turned in her seat, met his gaze, and subtly winked. He nodded back, giving her a small smile. She then bent to whisper in Cami's ear, who whispered to Nora.

"Those three redheads have to be her sisters, am I right?" his mom asked softly.

"Yep."

The night before, he'd been dragged out to dinner by the sisters and interrogated. That had been interesting. He'd had an are-you-good-enough grilling from a woman's father before, but never her posse of younger sisters. They were good girls, and he could see a lot of Anne's no-nonsense demeanor and world-class sense of humor had rubbed off on them.

They'd also promised to *take care of* their mother for Anne and him. He'd tried not to get an ominous chill over how they intended to go about that, but in cases like this, maybe it was better not to ask questions.

The ceremony was thankfully short, the bridal party filed out to be quickly waylaid by the photographer, and everyone else rose to walk the fifty feet to the banquet hall where the reception was being held. One wall of the building was made of glass doors that were thrown open to let the ocean breeze in and let the guests out on the deck to take in the view. A DJ was set up inside, already playing some slow tunes and encouraging people to dance. A few couples were out on the floor, swaying to the beat. Apparently, Meg and Finn weren't big on the formality of people standing around watching them do the first dances. That was fine with Gabe. He wasn't a fan of formality either. Buffet tables were set up with glasses of the bubbly and trays of tiny hors d'oeuvres. Gabe and his family got some food and drinks and went out to lean against the deck railing.

"You okay?" His dad glanced at him.

He took a fortifying swig of champagne. "I was less nervous on my first date."

David snorted. "Little brother, you went out with a hot senior cheerleader on your first date. And you were a sophomore."

"I know. This is worse." This actually mattered in a long-term, rest of his life kind of way. He had no idea how Anne would react to him showing up here. He hoped she'd be pleasantly surprised, but she had a habit of catching him off-guard.

Had she thought about him in the last ten days? Had she woken up in the middle of the night, reaching for him the way he'd reached for her? Had the loneliness been eating her alive, even though she was surrounded by people? He'd suffered through a one-week cruise on the *Alaskan Adventure*, then he'd told the cruise company he needed to be gone for the three-week cruise after that. He'd promised to return to finish up the season, but he hoped it was with the knowledge that Anne would be waiting for him when he was done.

"It looks like the photographer just wrapped up." His sister-in-law grinned, sipping a glass of ginger ale. "This is exciting. She must be really special for you to fly us all in for this."

"She is, and thanks for coming on short notice." Gabe blew out a breath. Seeing Anne had only made him more certain of what he wanted—her, in his life, always—but he needed to know if she still felt the same way she had in Alaska.

"Gabe, turn around." His mom ordered, and he pivoted without thinking.

There she was, so precious and beautiful she made his heart ache. He stepped forward, his feet carrying him across the distance that separated them. He was intensely aware of her friends, his family, and her sisters all watching with acute interest. She examined a stuffed mushroom and popped it in her mouth. The moment she glanced up and saw him, her eyes went wide, she sucked in a quick breath, and choked.

He reached out and thumped her between the shoulder blades, and she coughed the hors d'oeuvre into the napkin she held.

"Well," she wheezed. "That was elegant."

As if he cared about elegance. He rubbed a hand up and down her spine. "You okay?"

"I'm fine." She tossed the wadded napkin into a nearby trash can and turned to look at him squarely. Her gaze searched his face, but her expression was unreadable. "I'm...shocked to see you."

"Good shocked or bad shocked?" He braced himself for the answer.

"I—"

Their audience decided that was the moment to break in. Damn it. Julie stepped forward. "He called my shop, and I told Meg and Karen."

"So I invited him." Meg and her new husband stood hand-in-hand, looking entirely pleased with their part in this conspiracy.

The hugely pregnant friend, Karen, piped up. "It was pretty clear you were depressed from the moment you got home. We know you too well for you to hide it from us."

Anne closed her eyes. "I'm sorry, Meg. I didn't want to ruin your celebration."

"You didn't," the bride assured her. "But all of us wanted you to be happy today too, and you weren't. I thought importing a really hot wedding date for you would help. You're welcome."

A laugh straggled out of her and her eyes opened again. "Thanks...I think. I don't even...this wasn't..."

None of those things sounded particularly positive or promising, and Gabe's heart sank.

The sisters descended, and Cami blurted, "We evicted Mom this morning."

Anne's head snapped around and she stared at her youngest sibling. "Excuse me?"

Hazel folded her arms, chin jutting pugnaciously. "We had a little come-to-Jesus meeting with her, and then we told her she had one week to pack up her stuff and get the hell out of *your* house."

"How'd that go over?" Gabe's eyebrows arched. Well, that was better than he'd feared when they claimed they'd handle their mother.

"About as well as a nuclear bomb." Nora's expression was somber. "But we were serious and she knew it. We even got out boxes and started packing her up."

"Is that why she had a sudden headache and couldn't make it to my wedding?" Meg asked.

"Yep. That, and she was hoping to make us feel guilty enough to ruin our day too. Or maybe just guilt us into staying there to pamper her in her hour of need." Cami pushed her retro cat-eye glasses up the bridge of her nose and shrugged. "Whatever. It didn't work."

Groaning quietly, Anne rubbed a fingertip between her eyebrows. "That's going to be a fun meltdown to go home to."

Hazel shook her head. "Nope, you're not going home until she's gone. You can stay with one of your friends—"

"Or with Gabe." Cami grinned, flashing dimples. "He's staying at the Bayside Inn with his family. I've always thought that was the cutest

B&B in town."

"Back to the point." Nora met Anne's gaze, something resolute, angry, and sad molding her features. "You've put up with Mom's crap for *us* since Dad died. We'll handle this for you. When you come home, you'll have a drama-mama-free house."

Cami added, "She didn't bother to raise us, and if it weren't for you, we'd have been so hosed growing up. But we're adults now, and we can fend for ourselves. Mom needs to do the same. She's *not* your responsibility, and she has no right to act like she's given up so much to raise the four of us. That's bullcrap, and we read her every kind of riot act about her behavior toward you and us."

"That part was kind of fun," Hazel admitted. She seemed to be the quietest of the three, but no less determined to help Anne.

"It really was." Nora cracked a smile. "Her sense of entitlement blows my mind, but it stops now. So, Anne, if you want to run away with Gabe, you don't have to worry about Mom. She's going to have to start taking care of herself."

"Or find someone else to enable her, which is more likely." Cami rolled her eyes. "I'm guessing we have a new stepdaddy in the next year."

Nora and Hazel looked equal parts annoyed and nauseated by that idea.

Cami steamrolled right along. "For the record, I like Gabe."

"We had dinner with him last night." Hazel bit her lip. "We threatened to kill him if he wasn't good to you, Anne. Nora used some very medical sounding terms to tell him she'd cut off his dick if he behaved like a dick. And he seemed to think that was fair. Or at least he didn't run screaming. So, you can keep him...he's nice."

"And hot." Cami waggled her eyebrows. "You were all thinking it."

"Yep." Nora laughed, grabbed her baby sister's arm, and towed her toward the buffet tables.

"Absolutely." Hazel hid a grin behind her water glass. "I'm going to go see if Karen's brother wants to dance. That'll bug Nora, don't you think?"

Silence fell after the sisters left, and Gabe cleared his throat. "I take it Nora doesn't get along with Karen's brother."

"A long-standing feud, unfortunately." Karen shook her head and sighed.

Anne still didn't say anything. Her gaze went from her departing sisters, to her friends, to his family, to him. Her lips trembled and she looked like she was about to lose her cool. Her cheeks flushed, and he could see a hint of tears in her eyes. He knew she'd hate crying in front of a crowd of wedding guests, and he couldn't bear seeing her so upset. Everyone was pushing her toward him, emotions were high, and she needed some breathing room.

"Dance with me." He didn't wait for an answer, just grabbed her hand and hauled her out to the dance floor.

He pulled her close, they moved together, and it felt so *good* to hold her again. Soft strands of her hair brushed his jaw and cheek, her scent filled his nose, and her breasts and thighs brushed against him with every step.

She took a few jerky little breaths, her fingers digging into his shoulders.

"Shh." He smoothed his palm in circles along her spine. "Deep breaths, honey. It's going to be okay."

Something remarkably close to a sob emerged. "I don't...I don't know..."

"Despite what everyone's said, you don't need to know anything right now. You don't have to run away from home or agree with your friends and sisters." He pulled her closer. "Just dance with me."

Little by little, she relaxed against him, swaying to the beat. Gabe never wanted this song to end because he wasn't sure he'd survive when it came time to face the music. He'd do whatever it took to keep her, but that only worked if she was willing to compromise to make something real and permanent happen between them. He hoped she'd be willing to listen when he apologized for demanding she give up her entire existence for him. He still thought he was right about what would make her happy, but that was her choice to make, not his.

He only prayed she made a choice he could live with.

B eing in his embrace felt so damn amazing, it made Anne's eyes well with tears. The cessation of pain was so sharp, it was almost too much to bear. She moved with him, and it felt as natural as breathing. The last ten days had sucked on a level she didn't like to admit, but she refused to lie to herself. She'd barely managed to go through the motions.

Just hold it together, just smile like you're happy to be back, just try not to screw up your friends' happy moments. That had been her mantra lately. Finn and Meg had their wedding. Karen and Tate were about to have their baby. Lukas and Julie were moving in together.

Their contentment oozed around her, but she didn't feel it herself. She'd been smothered under a blanket of wonderfulness she couldn't quite internalize. She'd known her friends could tell something was up, but other than the occasional sideways glance, they'd left her alone. Now she knew why, since they were planning to spring Gabe on her at the reception.

She'd thought her mother's nonstop drama had kept her sisters too preoccupied to notice anything was wrong with Anne. It was one of the few times she'd thanked God for Dinah. Her ability to keep the sisters distracted was probably the only thing that had spared the drama llama's life this past week.

Though it appeared she didn't need to worry about her mom anymore. There was no need to figure out how to have The Talk. Her sisters had taken care of it for her. There was a certain irony to the daughters Dinah hadn't bothered to raise handing her ass to her. It wasn't nice, but Anne smiled against Gabe's chest as they danced. Hey, she deserved a bit of *Schadenfreude* after everything her mom had pulled. She was just glad that the dirty work of evicting Dinah hadn't fallen to her. She owed her sisters one.

She apparently also owed her besties one for hooking her up with a hot wedding date. "Hey, Gabe?"

"Yeah?" He swept his hand up her back, and a sweet tingle broke out everywhere he touched.

"It was good shocked, for the record."

It took a moment for him to react, and then his breath whooshed out. "Thank *God.*"

A short laugh escaped her. "It doesn't solve anything though, does it?"

"Look, I was a pushy jackass that last night. I threw out an all-or-nothing deal to you, and that was wrong. You have every right to decide what kind of job you should have, and whatever reasons you have for keeping that job are your own. I have no business critiquing that." His fingers toyed with the short curls at the base of her neck. "Be a teacher, be whatever you want. I'll support you one hundred percent. What's most important to me is that you're willing to make a relationship work between us."

A sigh slipped from her throat, so many conflicting emotions colliding within her that she didn't know what to say first. "Long-distance?"

"Sometimes, yeah." Worry tightened his features, though they still moved to the music. "But I can base myself in Half Moon Bay, take shorter guide trips in California. You've got plenty of wilderness here. I've done some work in the Sierra Nevadas before, so...why not more? Maybe you could come with me to Alaska during the summers. Or something. No pressure. We'll be apart some of the time, but I'll be with you as often as possible. Or we can work out another compromise that gives us both what we need."

He was nervous. Gabe, the king of confidence, was stumbling over his words in his rush to convince her to give him a chance. Her heart squeezed with so much love, and she pressed her palms to his chest. "You've put a lot of thought into this."

"I've haven't done much else for the last ten days." He lifted one hand to cup her jaw. "Being without you blew. Hard."

She couldn't hold back a cheeky grin. "I've always thought blowing you was fun."

The corners of his eyes crinkled in wry amusement. "Tease."

"Is it a tease, or a promise for later?" She tried for an innocent expression, but doubted she pulled it off.

He stroked a thumb over her cheek. "Is that a yes to a relationship?"

She sobered, meeting his gaze frankly. "It's more complicated than that. You weren't the only one who's had a lot of time to think since we parted."

"Okay." He nodded, urging her on, though she could read the trepidation in his eyes.

Gathering up every ounce of courage she had, she confessed what she hadn't managed to tell anyone else. Not even her best friends.

"I..." Her mouth dried. She licked her lips and tried again. "I don't want to teach PE anymore. I love my students, but I never wanted to be a middle school teacher. This career doesn't make me happy. And I've *earned* some happiness."

"I couldn't agree more." Not a hint of triumph showed on his face, just concern and sympathy for her struggle, even though she'd basically said he'd been right all along. "You don't need to be a teacher anymore, just for the sake of having a steady monthly income. Your sisters are more than capable of taking care of themselves *because* of all the sacrifices you made for them."

She made a face, hoping she wasn't blushing under the blatant admiration in his gaze. "I didn't—"

He tugged on her earlobe. "Maybe you think it was no big deal, or just doing the right thing, but allow me to consider you amazing if I want to."

"Okay. Twist my arm."

"That's my girl." He cradled her closer. "You deserve to be happy."

Yes, and while taking care of her sisters had been fulfilling, it hadn't been an easy path to follow. "I would have been miserable leaving my sisters behind, knowing they weren't being taken care of the way my dad would have wanted, knowing my mom was just going to be overwhelmed and unable to cope. Sticking around meant we could all get what we needed. Family means everything to me."

"Me too. Though they've never needed me like yours needed you."

"That's life." She shrugged. "You have a really nice family."

"I'm willing to share. My mom and dad adore you." He nodded to a blond couple dancing not far from them, the man resembling Gabe so much he had to be the older brother. "I'm sure David and Raquel will adore you too. I'll introduce you to them later."

His parents were also dancing nearby, casting them occasional glances, but not interfering. Vince smiled at her and Peggy gave her an encouraging thumbs up. Anne chuckled. It was really cool that his whole family had shown up to support him. She arched her eyebrows at Gabe. "Well, I'm adorable, what can I say?"

"You are." His gaze was so filled with tenderness it made moisture well in her eyes. He pulled her closer. "I love you, Anne."

"Ah, damn." A tear escaped and she swiped at it. "I love you too. I tried so hard not to, but I do anyway."

He winced. "Because you hated my job."

"I *love* your job way too much, but everything about your life scares me. It just smacks of my mother's brand of irresponsibility. I've worked my ass off to bring some stability to my sisters' and my lives." The right thing and the smart thing were still at odds, and she hadn't yet figured out how to reconcile them in a way she could live with. "Your occupation doesn't have that stability or financial security."

He blew out a breath. "Those things are important, I agree."

Maybe he agreed in theory. She gave him a look. "I don't see you going back to being a Silicon Valley programmer."

"Never," he concurred.

"I wouldn't want you to. I love you just the way you are. But I don't know how there can be any compromise for *me*. For us, yes. I want a relationship, I'm willing to make it work, even if it means we aren't together all the time."

His eyes slid closed and he pressed his forehead against hers. His voice turned husky with emotion. "I love you. We can work anything else out, I swear."

"I love you too." She wasn't as sure they could work out her job issues, but she had no doubts about them as a couple. Having him leave on trips she would *love* to join him on wouldn't be fun on several levels, but if the other option was living without him...no contest.

He pulled back and seemed to gird himself, and his gaze was a little wary when he looked at her. "So, if money was no object, would you want to join me as a guide?"

She snorted. "Hell, yes."

"No hesitation?"

"None." But since independently wealthy wasn't something that was possible on a teacher's salary, she didn't see how the question mattered.

"Okay, then we're all set." He nodded crisply.

She pursed her lips. "How's that, Camper Guru?"

Rolling his eyes, he didn't bother to hide his pique. "If I have a solution that even *you* can't argue with, do you promise never to call me that again?"

She thought about it for at least thirty seconds longer than was really necessary. Keeping him in suspense, just for sheer fun and he knew it. He jostled her a bit.

"Okay, okay. I promise."

The wariness came back full force. "Programmers make a nice salary, you know."

"Yeah." Duh. She didn't say the last part, but she knew he heard it anyway.

He narrowed his eyes, but said nothing about her tone. "And you know I've done some programming on the side since I quit the rat race."

"Yeah. Are we getting to the point now?"

"I'm getting there, I promise." He dipped her over his arm and twirled her around in a quick step. She laughed, clutching at his shoulders. Taking advantage, he popped a kiss on her mouth. "I've patented some of the software I've created. And I turned my savings over to my brother and sister-in-law. They've taken good care of my money, investing it and stuff."

"Okay." She slipped her arms around his waist, pressing herself into his hard angles. She was starting to lose interest in the conversation. It had been *days* since he'd kissed her properly, touched her skin, rocked her world in bed.

Lust flushed his face, his hands curving over her hips. "I'm rich, Anne. I have around twenty million in the bank right now, and that doesn't include what my brother has plugged into various companies and stocks."

She froze, standing stock still in the middle of the dance floor. "Are you being serious right now?"

"Dead serious." He shrugged, almost bashful about his wealth. "If you marry me, what's mine is yours, you know. That means you don't have to worry about retirement. I always have enough set aside that even if every investment went belly up, I'd still be set for life. So *we'd* be set for life." He held up his hands as if warding off a protest she hadn't made. "I know you wouldn't love being dependent on my money though, so I've spoken to David and Raquel and they'll invest what *you* make from guiding so you have your own nest egg. They had some crazy ideas about us starting our own outdoor adventures business, but we'll figure that stuff out later. Just...if you want to run off to the wilderness with me, you will *not* end up destitute."

He'd dragged all that out? If he'd said this back in Alaska, she wouldn't have been twisting herself into knots for over a week. But the annoyance was a mere spark to the joy that exploded deep inside her. He really had found a way to give her everything she could ever want, everything that would make her happy. A sob ripped out of her, and she slammed the pointy toe of her shoe into his shin.

"Ow, damn." He flinched, hunching to grab his leg.

She launched herself at him, twined her arms around his neck, and kissed him hard. Though he stumbled a bit to catch his balance, he was quick on the recovery and then hauled her closer. Their lips fused, a fiery reunion they'd both craved, and love and desire welled inside her with equal ferocity. His arms were steel bands around her, holding her tight, but his lips worshipped hers slowly and very, very thoroughly. Their tongues met, and the flavor of him filled her mouth. Champagne and sugar and Gabe. Nothing had ever been sweeter or more perfect. She was never going to get enough of this man, and she couldn't be more thrilled about it. Somehow, everything had worked out well. She would never have guessed it possible, but here she was, *exactly* where she wanted to be, and with nothing but a promising future stretching out before her.

They were both breathing hard when he pulled back to ask, "Does this mean you'll marry me?"

"Hell, yes." She poked his chest. "Someone has to keep you out of trouble."

He laughed, looking every bit as ecstatic as she felt. "Or get me into it."

"That too." Grinning against his lips, she said, "We're gonna have a lot of fun, Gabe."

Dimples flashing, he rocked her in his embrace. "The adventure of a lifetime, sweetheart. I promise."

Game on.

THE END

Want more from C. Jordan? Sign up for her newsletter:
https://www.cjordanbooks.com/newsletter

ABOUT C. JORDAN

C. Jordan is a California native with an insatiable love for travel. When she's not writing sexy contemporary romance, she can usually be found working as a librarian or wandering the world with her husband.

ALSO BY C. JORDAN

Destination: Desire series

A Little Sinful

Never Let Go

Maybe This Time

Wild For You

Forrester Brothers series

A Girl's Best Friend

The Girl Next Door

Unbelievable series

If You Believe

Believe in Me

Make Me Believe

Unbelievable anthology

Revved Up series

All Revved Up

All Tangled Up

Revved Up duology

EXCERPT FROM
GETTING IT RIGHT

Half Moon Bay, California

"Thanks for lending me a hand, Ben." Laurel Patton stepped back, propped her fists on her hips, and surveyed their handiwork. She stood in the middle of her brother and sister-in-law's living room, looking at a pair of paintings hanging over their couch. One had been there for years, the second was a gift for their eleventh anniversary.

"No problem." Her sister-in-law's younger brother grinned conspiratorially, dimples digging deep grooves into his cheeks.

Ben had helped her sneak into the house while Tate and Karen were out. The two collaborators had hauled the sizeable canvas in from Laurel's car and positioned the pieces so they hung evenly on the wall.

Her original watercolor of Positano on the Amalfi Coast of Italy had captured the way the town's pastel buildings layered up the side of a cliff like a fancy wedding cake. It was where Tate had first introduced the Patton family to Karen, and where he'd proposed to her. Beside it now hung a painting of the house the couple had bought and restored a few years back—a gingerbread-laden Victorian mansion perched on a bluff over the Pacific Ocean. Laurel had tried to evoke the same style and palette, so that the two canvases were obviously meant to be a pair. Since she didn't work with watercolor very often anymore, it had been a nice challenge to her artistic skills.

She tilted her head and eyed her work critically. Not too bad. The first painting was done while she was taking a watercolor class as part of her Fine Arts degree from the Rhode Island School of Design. She'd loved her years at RISD, and trying to recapture that frame of mind for the new canvas had taken her back to those times.

Ben bumped his shoulder against hers. "They're going to love it. It blows my gift to them out of the water."

"Thanks." She winked. "I like kicking everyone else's ass with my awesomeness."

He snorted. "Your modesty slays me."

"You're welcome." She turned to walk into the kitchen, going to the fridge for a bottle of water. It was probably her last chance to get anything before the catering company took over for the anniversary party that night.

Ben followed and settled back against the enormous island, shoving his hands in his suit pockets. He looked every inch the ambitious young lawyer now, but he'd still been in his gawky teen years the first time they'd met.

All grown up now, he'd just passed his bar exam and joined her brother's firm the month before, and she'd bet Ben would be stellar in the courtroom with his resonant bass voice that could rival James Earl Jones. Considering his voice had cracked on every other word when they'd been introduced, she'd been pleasantly surprised his tone had deepened so much. No one wanted a squeaky-voiced lawyer defending them.

She waved her bottle at him. "What did you get our siblings?"

He cocked his head. "It sounds a little incestuous when you say *our* siblings, even if it is technically correct."

"What did you get my brother and sister-in-law, aka your sister and brother-in-law?" She rolled her eyes. "It was faster my way."

"A date night while I babysit Nick. They get gift certificates for a movie and dinner at their favorite restaurant."

Pursing her lips, she nodded. "That's a pretty good gift. I think any couple with a rambunctious toddler would love that."

"Yeah, but it's not a piece of art from a famous painter." He widened his eyes as if to indicate any idiot would agree with him.

"Pfft. Fame is relative. I'm not exactly Van Gogh."

"Says the woman who got invited to be an artist-in-residence at The Creative Enclave." He wagged a finger at her. "Don't think Tate wasn't bragging about you after you told him that."

She felt a rush of heat hit her cheeks. Her, Laurel Patton, blushing. There was a novel experience. Of course, she blew any semblance of modesty by offering a cocky grin and throwing her hands up in victory. "I am a badass, what can I say?"

"Tate pulled up their website and read the list of names for artists who've been part of their program." He gave a low whistle. "You're in some august company there."

"Some of my idols have been artist-in-residence for The Enclave. Okay...the idols who were around during the last century. I have some that have been dead since the Renaissance." She took a swig of water. "It'll be a whole summer of painting. Plus, I get to mentor an up-and-coming painter too. I've taught a few art classes over the years, but never individual mentoring. It should be fun. Unless they're an asshole, in which case I will make their lives miserable for three months. Because: homework."

"That's the spirit." He winked. "Always have a strategy for winning."

"I like winning," she agreed. Part of the fun of this trip was that she would get to spend time with other artists. Not just painters, but sculptors, potters, photographers, videographers, writers...you name it. She liked the idea of having that kind of community, at least for a while. Painting was a pretty solitary profession.

"When do you leave?"

"Tate's driving me to SFO in the morning. I just have to survive this party." She couldn't hold in a deep sigh, some of her excitement fizzling away.

"Your parents are coming, huh?" Sympathy reflected in his gaze.

"Let's be honest. It'll be just my mother. Daddy Dearest isn't taking the time to come to a party with no political gain. The guest list isn't A-list enough."

Ben winced, but didn't deny it. They both knew Robert Patton had worked Tate like a dog for years, trying to remake his son in his image, and it had nearly cost Tate his marriage. Laurel was grateful her brother had seen the light of day before he's lost the best thing that had ever happened to him. Karen was an absolute gem. Laurel had liked her on sight, somehow knowing this woman would be the only thing Tate loved more than the law. Well, now he had Karen, little Nick, and then the law. Which was how it should be.

Ben injected a note of cheer into his voice. "Well, my parents will both be here and they rock."

"I know, you lucky bastard," she groused.

He just laughed.

Dear God, she was going to have to deal with her mother. The two of them always brought out the absolute worst in each other.

Francesca, the obnoxious socialite who insisted her daughter marry the right sort of man, and Laurel, whose inner rebellious teen came out with claws bared.

"I notice you got your hair dyed again." Ben's grin turned wicked. "I like the turquoise streaks—very fluorescent. Your mom's going to love it."

"Yep." She fluffed her long tresses, not bothering to deny that needling her mother had been part of the decision-making process for refreshing her always colorful hair. She'd done green, blue, purple, fire engine red...pick a neon shade. It was her signature now. Sometimes she did streaks and sometimes she dyed only the tips. One time, she'd done just the left side of her head bright pink. Francesca's eyeballs had nearly exploded out of their sockets when she'd seen the effect. Watching the apoplectic reaction had been awesome. Laurel grinned at the memory. "Let the games begin."